Maigret and the Black Sheep

Maigret and

Translated from the French by Helen Thomson

Georges Simenon

the **Black** Sheep

A Helen and Kurt Wolff Book

 Harcourt Brace Jovanovich

New York and London

Library of Congress Cataloging in Publication Data

Simenon, Georges, 1903–
  Maigret and the black sheep.

  Translation of Maigret et les braves gens.
  "A Helen and Kurt Wolff book."
  I. Title.
PZ3.S5892Maegb [PQ2637.I53] 843'.9'12 75–20384

ISBN 0–15–155146–4

First American edition

#14012   3/76
B C D E

Maigret and the Black Sheep

1

Instead of groaning as he usually did when the telephone rang in the middle of the night and he groped for the receiver in the dark, Maigret heaved a sigh of relief.

He could no longer remember clearly what he had been dreaming about when the telephone rang, but he knew that it had been an unpleasant dream: he had been trying to explain to somebody important, whose face he couldn't make out and who was extremely displeased with him, that it wasn't his fault, that he had to be patient with him, patient for a few days only, because he was out of practice and felt restless and uncomfortable. Rely on him and it wouldn't take long. Above all, don't eye him reproachfully, ironically . . .

"Hello . . ."

As he drew the receiver to his ear, Madame Maigret, propping herself up on her elbow, switched on the bedside light.

"Maigret?" asked the caller.

3

"Yes."

He did not recognize the voice although it sounded familiar.

"It's Saint-Hubert . . ."

A police superintendent about his own age, whom he had known from the start of his career. They called each other by their last names, but did not use the familiar "tu." Saint-Hubert was tall and thin, a redhead, rather slow and formal and anxious to score points.

"Did I wake you up?"

"Yes."

"I'm so sorry. Anyway, any minute now I think you'll get a call from the Quai des Orfèvres to tell you about it, as I've alerted the District Attorney and Police Headquarters."

Maigret, sitting on his bed, took from the bedside table a pipe which he had allowed to go out when he went to sleep. He looked around for some matches. Madame Maigret got some for him from the mantelpiece. The window was open: Paris was still warm, dotted with lights, and one could hear taxis passing in the distance.

This was the first time they had been awakened like this since their return from vacation five days ago, and for Maigret it was something of a renewed contact with reality, with routine.

"I'm listening," he murmured as he puffed at his pipe while his wife held the burning match above the bowl.

"I'm in the apartment of Monsieur René Josselin, 37B Rue Notre-Dame-des-Champs, just next door to the convent of the Little Sisters of the Poor . . . A crime has just been discovered which I don't know much about as I only arrived some twenty minutes ago . . . Can you hear me?"

"Yes . . . "

Madame Maigret went into the kitchen to make some coffee and Maigret winked at her in approval.

"It seems a confusing case, and very likely a tricky one . . . That's why I have taken the liberty of calling you. I was afraid they would just send one of the officers on duty."

He was choosing his words and it was obvious that he was not alone in the room.

"I knew that you had been on vacation recently."

"I came back last week."

It was Wednesday. Or rather Thursday, since the hands of the alarm clock on Madame Maigret's bedside table showed that it was ten minutes past two in the morning. They had both gone to the movies, not so much to see the film, which was run-of-the-mill, as to get back into their routine.

"Are you going to come?"

"As soon as I put some clothes on."

"I would appreciate it. I know the Josselin family slightly. One wouldn't expect a tragedy like this to happen in the home of such people . . . "

Even the smell of tobacco was a professional smell: that of a pipe, put out the previous evening and relit in the middle of the night after being awakened by an emergency call. The coffee too had a different aroma to morning coffee. And the smell of gasoline that came through the open window.

For the past week Maigret had felt as if he were floundering. For once they had stayed for three whole weeks at Meung-sur-Loire, without any contact at all with Police Headquarters, without being called back to Paris on an urgent case, as had happened in previous years.

They had continued to fix up the house and garden. Maigret had gone fishing, had played *belote* with the locals, and ever since his return he hadn't managed to get back into his daily routine.

And neither had Paris, so it seemed. It had not rained or become cooler, as was usual after the holiday season. Large sightseeing cars were still touring the streets thronged with foreigners in multi-colored shirts, and although many Parisians had returned, many were still leaving by the trainful.

Police Headquarters, the office, seemed rather unreal to Maigret who sometimes wondered what he was doing there, as if his real life was far away on the banks of the Loire.

This unsettled feeling had doubtless given rise to his dream, the details of which he tried to remember without success. Madame Maigret came out of the kitchen with a hot cup of coffee and realized immediately that her husband, far from being annoyed by this rude awakening, was relieved.

"Where did it happen?"

"In Montparnasse . . . Rue Notre-Dame-des-Champs . . . "

He had put on his shirt, his trousers; he was lacing his shoes when the telephone rang again. This time it was Police Headquarters.

"This is Torrence, Chief . . . We've just been informed that . . ."

6

"That a man has been killed on Rue Notre-Dame-des-Champs . . ."

"You already know? Will you be going?"

"Who is in the office?"

"There's Dupeu, who's interrogating a suspect in the jewel theft case, then there's Vacher . . . Wait . . . Lapointe is just coming back now . . ."

"Tell him to go and wait for me there . . ."

Janvier was on vacation. Lucas, who had come back the day before, had not yet returned to work at the Quai.

"Shall I call a taxi?" asked Madame Maigret a little later.

Downstairs, he found a driver who recognized him and for once this pleased him.

"Where do I take you, Chief?"

He gave the address, filled a new pipe. On the Rue Notre-Dame-des-Champs he saw a small black car belonging to Police Headquarters and Lapointe standing on the sidewalk smoking a cigarette as he chatted to a policeman.

"Third floor on the left," announced the latter.

Maigret and Lapointe went through the door of a well-kept, middle-class apartment house and saw a light on in the concierge's apartment; through the net curtain the Superintendent thought he recognized an inspector from the sixth *arrondissement* who was questioning the concierge.

The elevator had only just stopped when a door opened and Saint-Hubert came forward to greet them.

"The District Attorney's men won't be here for

7

another half-hour . . . Come in . . . You'll understand why I was anxious to telephone you."

They went into a large hall, then Saint-Hubert pushed open a door which was ajar and they came into a quiet living room, empty except for the body of a man slumped in a leather armchair. Fairly tall and rather fat, the body was crumpled up and the head, with the eyes open, was hanging to one side.

"I asked the family to go into another room . . . Madame Josselin is in the hands of the family doctor, Dr. Larue, who happens to be a friend of mine."

"Has she been wounded?"

"No. She wasn't here when the accident occurred. I will tell you briefly what I have been able to find out so far."

"Who lives in the apartment? How many people?"

"Two . . . "

"You spoke of a family . . ."

"You'll see . . . Monsieur and Madame Josselin have been living alone since their daughter got married. She married a young doctor, Dr. Fabre, a pediatrician who is assistant to Professor Baron at the Children's Hospital."

Lapointe was taking notes.

"This evening Madame Josselin and her daughter went to the Madeleine theater . . ."

"And the husbands?"

"René Josselin stayed by himself for awhile."

"Didn't he like the theater?"

"I don't know. I tend to think he didn't really like going out in the evenings."

8

"What did he do?"

"For the last two years, nothing. Before that he owned a cardboard factory on Rue du Saint-Gothard. He manufactured cardboard boxes, in particular fancy boxes for perfume dealers, for example. . . . He gave up the business because of his health."

"How old was he?"

"Sixty-five or sixty-six. So last night he was alone. Then his son-in-law joined him, I don't know exactly when, and the two men played chess."

Indeed, on a small table they could see a chessboard on which the pieces remained set out as if the game had been interrupted.

Saint-Hubert spoke in a low voice and they heard movements in other rooms whose doors were not completely closed.

"When the two women came back from the theater . . ."

"At what time?"

"At a quarter past twelve . . . As I was saying, when they came back, they found René Josselin in the state that you see him . . ."

"How many bullets?"

"Two . . . Two near the heart.

"Didn't the other tenants hear anything?"

"Their next-door neighbors are still on vacation."

"Were you notified right away?"

"No. They first called Dr. Larue who lives close by on Rue d'Assas and who was treating Josselin. That took some time and it was not until ten past one that I had a telephone call from my police station to say they had just been notified. I jumped into my

9

clothes, rushed here . . . I only asked a few questions since it was difficult to do otherwise with Madame Josselin in the condition I found her . . ."

"And the son-in-law?"

"He arrived shortly before you did."

"What does he say?"

"We had difficulty getting hold of him and ended up finding him at the hospital where he had gone to see a small boy suffering from encephalitis, if I understood correctly . . ."

"Where is he now?"

"In there . . ."

Saint-Hubert pointed to one of the doors. They could hear people whispering.

"From the little I've learned, there has been no theft and no signs of breaking-and-entering. . . The Josselins have no enemies . . . They're good people who lived quietly."

There was a knock at the door. It was Ledent, a young police surgeon whom Maigret knew and who shook his hand warmly before putting his case on a chest of drawers and opening it.

"The District Attorney telephoned me," he said. "Their representative is on the way."

"I would like to ask the young woman a few questions," murmured Maigret, whose eyes had scanned the room several times.

He understood Saint-Hubert's feeling. The room was not only elegant and comfortable, but gave a sense of peacefulness, of family life. It was not a formal living room; it was a room in which people enjoyed living; one felt that each item of furniture had its own function and history.

The huge tan-colored leather armchair, for instance, was obviously the chair in which René Josselin used to sit every evening. And directly across the room, the television set stood right in his field of vision.

The grand piano had been used for years by a little girl whose portrait hung on the wall and, near another armchair, not as deep as the one belonging to the head of the family, was an attractive Louis XV work table.

"Shall I call her?"

"I would prefer to see her in another room."

Saint-Hubert knocked at a door, disappeared for a moment, and came back to get Maigret who caught a glimpse of a bedroom and a man leaning over a woman lying on a bed.

Another woman, considerably younger, came up to him and said in a low voice:

"Would you come with me to my old room?"

A room which had remained a young girl's room, still filled with mementos, knick-knacks, photographs, just as if someone had wanted her to remember her younger days in her parents' home, even after her marriage.

"You're Superintendent Maigret, aren't you?"

He nodded.

"You may smoke your pipe . . . My husband smokes cigarettes from morning till night, except at the bedside of his young patients, of course."

She was wearing a rather smart dress and before going to the theater she had gone to the hairdresser. She was fiddling with a handkerchief.

"Do you prefer to stand?"

11

"Yes. And you would too, wouldn't you?"

She did not stay where she was, but paced up and down, not knowing where to look.

"I don't know if you can imagine the effect this has had . . . Every day you hear about crimes in the newspapers, on the radio, but you never think it can happen to you. Poor Daddy!"

"Were you very close to your father?"

"He was an exceptionally kind man. I was everything to him . . . I am his only child. Superintendent Maigret, you must try to find out what has happened, so that you can tell us . . . I can't stop thinking that it's all a terrible mistake . . ."

"Do you think the murderer could have got the wrong floor?"

She looked at him as if she were clinging to a life preserver, but suddenly shook her head.

"It's impossible . . . The lock hasn't been forced . . . My father must have opened the door . . ."

Maigret called out:

"Lapointe! You can come in."

Maigret introduced him and Lapointe blushed at finding himself in a young girl's bedroom.

"Allow me to ask you a few questions. Was it you or your mother who thought of going to the theater this night?"

"It's difficult to say. I think it was Mother. She is always the one who insists that I go out. I have two children, the oldest is three and the other is ten months old. When my husband isn't in his office, where I don't see him, he is away, either at the hospital or making house calls. He is totally dedicated to his profession. So, occasionally, two or three times a month, Mother phones and suggests I go out with her. There was a play on tonight that I wanted to see . . ."

"Wasn't your husband free?"

"Not until half past nine. That was too late. And besides, he doesn't like the theater . . ."

"When did you get here?"

"About half past eight."

"Where do you live?"

"On Boulevard Brune, near the Cité Universitaire . . . "

"Did you come by taxi?"

"No. My husband took me in his car. He had some time between two of his appointments."

"Did he come up?"

"He left me on the sidewalk."

"Was he planning to come back for you afterward?"

"That's usually the way we do it when my mother and I go out. Paul—that's my husband's name—used to join my father as soon as he had finished his rounds and they would play chess or watch television while they waited for us."

"Is that what happened last night?"

"According to what he has just told me, yes. He arrived shortly after half past nine. They began a game of chess. My husband then received a telephone call . . ."

"At what time?"

"He hasn't had time to tell me exactly when it

13

was. He left, and when Mother and I came back later we found what you see . . ."

"Where was your husband at that time?"

"I telephoned home immediately and Germaine, our maid, told me he hadn't come back."

"Didn't it occur to you to call the police?"

"I don't know . . . Mother and I were stunned. . . . We couldn't grasp it. . . . We needed someone to advise us and it was I who thought of calling Dr. Larue. . . . He is a friend, besides being Daddy's doctor . . ."

"Didn't your husband's absence surprise you?"

"At first I assumed he had been detained by an emergency. . . . Then when Dr. Larue arrived I telephoned the hospital . . . I managed to reach him there . . "

"What was his reaction?"

"He told me he would come right away . . . Dr. Larue had already called the police. I'm not sure if I am telling you all this in the right order . . . at the same time I was looking after Mother, who seemed completely dazed . . ."

"How old is she?"

"Fifty-one. She is much younger than Daddy who married late, at the age of thirty-five . . ."

"Would you send your husband in?"

With the door to the living room opened, Maigret could hear the voices of Mercier, the delegate from the D.A.'s office, and Etienne Gossard, a young coroner who, like the others, had been hauled out of bed. The men from Forensics would soon be taking over the living room.

14

"You sent for me?"

He was a young, thin, nervous man. His wife had come back with him and asked timidly:

"May I stay?"

Maigret nodded.

"I am told, Doctor, that you arrived here about half past nine."

"A little later, not much . . ."

"Had you finished your work?"

"I thought so, but in my profession you're never sure."

"I presume, when you leave home, you give your maid an address where you can be reached?"

"Germaine knew that I was here."

"She is your maid?"

"Yes. She looks after the children when my wife isn't there."

"How was your father-in-law?"

"The same as usual. He was watching television. It wasn't a very interesting program so he suggested a game of chess. We started to play. About a quarter past ten the telephone rang . . ."

"It was for you?"

"Yes. Germaine told me I was wanted urgently at 28 Rue Julie . . . That's in my district . . . Germaine hadn't heard the name clearly, Lesage or Lechat, or maybe Lachat . . . The person who had telephoned was apparently very excited . . ."

"Did you leave immediately?"

"Yes. I told my father-in-law that I would come back if my patient didn't keep me too long, and otherwise I would go straight home . . . That was

15

what I intended . . . I get up very early, because of the hospital . . . "

"How long did you stay with your patient?"

"There was no patient . . . I spoke to the concierge who looked at me in astonishment and told me that no one with a name like Lesage or Lachat lived in the building and that she didn't know of any sick child . . ."

"What did you do?"

"I asked her if I could telephone my home and I questioned Germaine again . . . She repeated that it was definitely number 28 Rue Julie . . . I rang the bells of numbers 18 and 38 on a random chance but with no success . . . Since I was already out I took the opportunity to stop by the hospital and see a small child I was worried about . . ."

"What time was that?"

"I don't know . . . I stayed nearly half an hour with the child . . . Then I made the rounds of the wards with one of the nurses . . . Finally someone came to tell me that my wife was on the telephone . . ."

"You are the last person to have seen your father-in-law alive. He didn't seem worried?"

"Not in the least. . . . As he showed me to the door he told me that he was going to finish the game alone. I heard him putting the chain on the door."

"Are you certain about that?"

"I heard the chain rattle as usual . . . I would swear to that."

"Therefore he must have opened the door to his murderer. . . . Tell me, Madame, when you arrived with your mother, I suppose the chain was not on?"

"How would we have gotten in?"

The doctor was taking small quick puffs at his cigarette, lighting one before he had finished the other, and was staring anxiously first at the carpet and then at the Chief Superintendent. He gave the impression of a man trying fruitlessly to solve a problem, and his wife was just as upset.

"I will have to go back over these questions in detail tomorrow. I am sorry . . ."

"I understand. . . ."

"Now I've got to see the men from Forensics."

"Are they going to take the body away?"

"They have to . . . "

No one mentioned the word autopsy but the young woman was obviously thinking about it.

"You may go back now to Madame Josselin. I will be in soon to see her for a moment; I'll keep the interview as brief as possible . . . "

In the living room Maigret mechanically shook the men's hands and greeted his colleagues from Forensics who were setting up their equipment.

The coroner, who was looking preoccupied, asked:

"What do you think, Maigret?"

"Nothing."

"Don't you think it's odd that someone actually called the son-in-law that evening to a patient who doesn't exist? How did he get on with his father-in-law?"

"I don't know."

He hated questions like this since they hardly came to pry into the intimacy of a family. The inspector whom Maigret had briefly glimpsed in the concierge's apartment came into the room, a notebook in his hand, and went up to Maigret and Saint-Hubert.

"The concierge is most explicit," he said. "I've been questioning her for nearly half an hour. She's a young, intelligent woman whose husband is a policeman. He's on duty tonight."

"What does she say?"

"She opened the door for Dr. Fabre at nine thirty-five. She is sure of the time, as she was about to go to bed and she set the alarm. She usually goes to bed early because her baby, who is only three months old, wakes her up very early in the morning for his first bottle . . .

"She was asleep at a quarter past ten, when her bell rang. She definitely recognized the voice of Dr. Fabre who gave his name as he went by . . . "

"How many people came and went afterward?"

"I'm getting to that. She tried to go back to sleep. She was just dozing off when someone rang the bell, in the street this time. The person who came in gave his name: Aresco—they're a South American family who live on the first floor. Almost immediately afterward the baby woke up. She tried unsuccessfully to get him back to sleep and ended up heating some sweetened water for him. No one came in or went out up to the time Madame Josselin and her daughter returned."

The inspectors, who had been listening, looked solemnly at each other.

"In other words," said the investigator, "Dr. Fabre is the last person to have left the house?"

"Madame Bonnet—that's the name of the concierge—is sure about this. If she had gone to sleep she might not be so certain. But because of the baby she was up the whole time . . ."

"Was she still up when the two women came back? Did the baby stay awake for two hours?"

"It seems so. She was, in fact, rather concerned and regretted not seeing Dr. Fabre when he returned, as she would have liked to ask his advice."

Everyone glanced inquisitively at Maigret, and the Chief Superintendent looked sullen.

"Have any empty cartridges been found?" he asked, turning toward one of the specialists from Forensics.

"Two cartridge shells . . . 6:35 . . . Can we take the body away?"

The men in white coveralls were waiting with the stretcher. Just as René Josselin passed through the door of his home, under a sheet, his daughter came quietly into the room. She caught Maigret's eye and he went up to her.

"Why did you come in?"

She did not answer him immediately. Her eyes followed the stretcher-bearers and the stretcher. Only when the door was closed did she whisper, almost as if speaking in a dream:

"An idea that crossed my mind . . . Wait . . ."

She walked toward an old chest of drawers which stood between the two windows and opened the top drawer.

"What are you looking for?"

Her lips were trembling as she gazed steadily, straight at Maigret.

"The gun . . ."

"Was there a gun in that drawer?"

"For years . . . That's why, when I was little, the drawer was always kept locked . . ."

"What sort of gun?"

"An automatic, very flat, bluish in color, with a Belgian trade-mark."

"A Browning 6:35?"

"I think so . . . I'm not sure . . . The word Herstal was engraved on it, as well as some numbers . . ."

The men looked at each other again, since the description corresponded to an automatic 6:35.

"When was the last time you saw it?"

"Quite some time ago . . . Some weeks . . . perhaps months . . . surely one night when we played cards, as the cards were kept in the same drawer . . . They are still there . . . Things stay in their place for a long time here . . ."

"But the automatic is not there now?"

"No."

"So whoever used it knew where to find it?"

"Perhaps my father took it to defend himself . . ."

Fear shone in her eyes.

"Your parents don't have a maid?"

"They had a maid who got married about six months ago. They have tried two others since then. Since Mother wasn't satisfied with them she hired a cleaning woman, Madame Manu. She comes at seven o'clock in the morning and leaves at eight at night."

All this was normal, everything was perfectly natural except for the fact that this quiet man, only recently retired, had been murdered in his armchair.

There was something disturbing, something incongruous about the incident.

"How is your mother?"

"Dr. Larue has forced her to lie down. She doesn't say a word and stares into space as if she weren't all there. She has not shed a single tear. She seems lost in a void . . . The doctor wants to know if you will let him give her a sedative . . . He wants her to sleep . . . May he?"

Why not? Maigret was not going to discover the truth by asking Madame Josselin a few questions.

"He may," he replied.

The men from Forensics were still working with their usual care and deliberation. The D.A.'s man decided to leave.

"Are you coming, Gossard? Have you got your car?"

"No. I came by taxi."

"I'll drive you back if you like."

Saint-Hubert left too, but not without having whispered to Maigret:

"Was I right to call you?"

The Chief Superintendent nodded and went to sit down in an armchair.

"Open the window," he said to Lapointe.

It was warm in the room and it suddenly surprised him that Josselin had spent the evening with all the windows shut in spite of the continuing summer temperatures.

"Bring in the son-in-law . . ."

"Right away, Chief . . ."

He came without delay, looking exhausted.

"Tell me, Doctor, were the windows open or closed when you left your father-in-law?"

He thought for a moment, looked at the two windows whose curtains were drawn.

"Wait . . . I don't know . . . I'm trying to remember . . . I was sitting here . . . I think I saw some lights . . . Yes . . . I could almost swear that the window on the left was open . . . I distinctly heard noises in the street."

"You didn't close the window before leaving?"

"Why should I have?"

"I don't know."

"No . . . It didn't occur to me . . . You forget that I am not in my own home."

"Did you come here often?"

"About once a week. Véronique visited her mother and father more often. Tell me . . . My wife is going to stay here tonight, but personally I would rather go home to bed. We never leave the children alone with the maid for the whole night. And besides, I must be at the hospital by seven tomorrow morning."

"What keeps you from leaving?"

He was surprised at this reply, as if he considered himself a suspect.

"Thank you . . . "

One could hear him speaking to his wife in the adjoining room. He then crossed the living room, bareheaded, his case in his hand, and self-consciously said good-by.

2

When the three men left the building only Madame
Josselin and her daughter remained in the apartment. The concierge's baby, after a restless night,
must have gone to sleep, for the room was in darkness and Maigret hesitated for a moment as he put
his finger to the bell.

"Doctor, what would you say to a drink?"

Lapointe, who was about to open the door of the
black car, left his hand where it was. Dr. Larue
looked at his watch, as if this would decide his reply.

"I'd gladly have a cup of coffee," he declared in the
same solemn, rather mellow voice that he used
when he was talking to his patients. "There must be
a café still open at the Montparnasse intersection."

It was not yet daylight. The streets were almost
deserted. Maigret looked up toward the third floor
and saw the light go off in the living room, where
one of the windows was still open.

Was Véronique Fabre at last going to undress and
go to bed in her old bedroom? Or would she stay be-

side her mother, now doped by the doctor's injection? What were her thoughts in these rooms suddenly empty, where so many strangers had recently been moving about?

"Bring the car . . ." the Chief Superintendent said to Lapointe.

They only had to go up Rue Vavin. Larue and Maigret went along the sidewalk. The doctor was rather small, broad-shouldered and chubby, a man who would never lose his composure, his dignity and gentleness. One could sense that he was accustomed to dealing with patients who were well-bred, financially comfortable and pampered, patients whose manners and tone of voice he had adopted and not without somewhat overdoing them.

In spite of his fifty odd years his blue eyes still had an expression of innocence and of fear of causing pain; Maigret was later to learn that he entered exhibits every year at the Salon des Peintres-Médecins.

"Have you known the Josselins for very long?"

"Ever since I settled in the district, that is to say for about twenty years. Véronique was still a little girl then, and unless I'm mistaken, it was when she had measles that they called me for the first time."

It was chilly, rather damp. A soft halo surrounded the gas burners. Several cars were parked outside a nightclub that was still open on the corner of Boulevard Raspail; the doorman in uniform in front of the entrance took the two men for potential customers and blasts of music burst forth as he pushed open the door.

Lapointe followed slowly behind them in the little car and parked at the curb.

Night life in Montparnasse had not quite ended. A couple were arguing in low voices by a wall near a hotel. In the café, whose lights were still on, as the doctor had thought, a few customers lingered and at the counter an old flower vendor was drinking a cup of coffee that smelled strongly of rum.

"I'll have a brandy and water," Maigret said.

The doctor hesitated.

"I think I'll have the same."

"And what about you, Lapointe?"

"The same for me, Chief."

"Three brandies and water . . . "

They sat at a small round table near the window and began to speak in undertones while the nightly activities of the café continued around them. Larue declared with conviction:

"They are decent people. They became friends of ours in no time and my wife and I often used to dine with them."

"Are they wealthy?"

"That depends what you mean by wealthy. They are certainly comfortable. René Josselin's father owned a small cardboard factory on Rue du Saint-Gothard, a simple workshop fitted with glass windows at the back of a yard, which employed about ten girls. When his son inherited it he bought modern equipment. He was a man of taste and imagination and pretty soon got the large perfume houses and other firms in the luxury business as clients."

"He appears to have married late, when he was about thirty-five?"

"That's right. He continued to live above the workshops on Rue du Saint-Gothard with his mother. She never enjoyed good health, and he did not hide the fact that it was because of her that he had not married sooner. On the one hand, he did not want to leave her alone. On the other, he did not feel he had the right to inflict the presence of a sick woman on a young wife. He worked hard, and lived only for his business."

"Cheers."

"Cheers."

Lapointe, his eyes red with fatigue, did not miss one word of the conversation.

"He married a year after his mother's death and moved to Rue Notre-Dame-des-Champs."

"Who was his wife?"

"Francine de Lancieux, the daughter of a retired colonel. I think they lived a few doors away, either on Rue du Saint-Gothard or Rue Dareau, and that's how Josselin knew her. She must have been twenty-two at the time."

"Did they get on well?"

"They were one of the most devoted couples I have known. They had a daughter almost at once, Véronique, whom you met tonight. Later they hoped for a son but an operation put an end to their dream."

Good people, the Police Superintendent had said, and now the doctor was saying the same thing. People with no complications, living in a quiet, comfortable setting.

"They came back from La Baule last week . . . they bought a villa there when Véronique was still a child and they continued to go there every year. Later, when Véronique had children of her own, they took her children there also."

"And the husband?"

"Dr. Fabre? I don't know if he ever took a vacation, and if he did it was probably not more than a week. Perhaps he joined them two or three times for a weekend. He's a man who devotes himself entirely to medicine and to his patients, a kind of lay saint. When he met Véronique he was an intern at the Children's Hospital and if he had not married he most probably would have been content with a hospital career, without worrying about a private practice."

"Do you think his wife insisted that he have an office?"

"I am not betraying a professional secret by answering that question. Fabre makes no secret of it. By devoting himself exclusively to hospital work he would have found it difficult to support a family. His father-in-law wanted him to purchase an office and advanced him the funds. He's not concerned with either his appearance or his comfort, as you have seen. His clothes are almost always crumpled, and left to himself, I wonder if he might not forget to change his underwear . . . "

"Did he get on well with Josselin?"

"The two men respected each other. Josselin was proud of his son-in-law and, apart from that, they had a mutual passion for chess."

"Was Josselin really ill?"

"It was I who asked him to slow down. He has always been overweight and I have known him to weigh almost two-hundred fifty pounds. That did not stop him from working twelve or thirteen hours a day. His heart wasn't keeping up. He had a fairly mild attack two years ago, but nonetheless it served as a warning.

"I advised him to take on an assistant and to limit his activity to some sort of supervision, just enough to keep his mind occupied.

"To my great surprise he preferred to retire completely, explaining that he was incapable of doing things half-way."

"So he sold his business?"

"To two of his employees. As they did not have enough money he kept an interest in it for a certain number of years, I can't remember exactly how many."

"What did he do with his time during the last two years?"

"In the morning he used to go for a stroll in the Luxembourg Gardens; I often saw him there. He would walk slowly, cautiously, like a lot of cardiacs, since he ended up by exaggerating his condition. He used to read a lot. You've seen his library. Never having had time to read before, he discovered literature late in life and spoke enthusiastically about it."

"And his wife?"

"In spite of the maid and then the cleaning woman when they decided not to have a live-in servant any more, she devoted considerable time herself to the house and the cooking. In addition she went almost every day to Boulevard Brune to see her grandchildren, and took the eldest in her car to Montsouris Park."

"You must have been surprised when you discovered what had happened?"

"It still hurts me to think it possible. I have seen some tragedies among my patients, not a lot, but some nevertheless. On each occasion one might have expected it. Do you know what I mean? In each case, despite appearances, there existed, like a chink in the armor, an element of trouble. This time I can't even guess . . ."

Maigret motioned to the waiter to fill up the glasses.

"What bothers me is Madame Josselin's reaction," the doctor went on, still with the same blandness. "Or rather, I would say her non-reaction, her total debility. I haven't been able to get a single sentence out of her all night. She looked at us, at her daughter, her son-in-law, and at me, as if she didn't see us. She has not shed one tear. From her room we could hear the noises in the living room. It was not difficult, with a little imagination, to piece together what was going on: the flashes from the photographers' cameras for example, then when the body was taken away . . .

"I thought that then, at least, she would react, try to rush in. She was conscious and yet she did not move, did not wince.

"She spent the greatest part of her life with a man and then suddenly, on her return from the theater, finds herself alone . . .

"I wonder how she will readjust . . ."

"Do you think her daughter will take her to her home?"

"It's hardly likely. The Fabres live in one of those

new buildings with fairly compact apartments. Though she loves her daughter and adores her grandchildren, I think she would find it difficult to live all the time with them. Now it's time I went home . . . tomorrow morning my patients will be waiting. . . . No, no . . . Let me . . ."

He had taken his wallet out of his pocket. The Chief Superintendent had been quicker than he.

People were coming out of the nightclub nearby, a whole group of musicians and dancers who were waiting for each other or were saying goodnight, and one could hear the clatter of high heels on the pavement.

Lapointe took his place at the wheel beside Maigret whose face was expressionless.

"Home?"

"Yes."

They were silent for awhile as the car passed through the empty streets.

"Early tomorrow morning I would like someone to go to Rue Notre-Dame-des-Champs and question the tenants of the building as they get up. It is possible that some people may have heard the gunshots and weren't concerned, thinking it was a car backfiring . . . I would also like to know the whereabouts of the tenants from half past nine onward . . ."

"I'll see to it myself, Chief."

"No. You will go off to bed after you have left instructions. If Torrence is available send him around to Rue Julie, to the three numbers whose bells Dr. Fabre claims to have rung."

"Right."

"Just to be on the safe side, we'd better verify the time of his arrival at the hospital . . ."

"Is that all?"

"Yes . . . Yes and no . . . I have the feeling I am forgetting something; for the last quarter of an hour at least I have been wondering what . . . It's just an impression, a hint that's come to me several times during the night . . . At a certain moment something alerted me, and then someone spoke to me, Saint-Hubert if I'm not mistaken . . . By the time I had replied I simply could not remember what I had begun thinking about . . ."

They reached Boulevard Richard-Lenoir. The bedroom window was still open onto the darkness, just like the Josselins' living-room window had been after the men from the D.A.'s office had left.

"Goodnight, son."

"Goodnight, Chief."

"I doubt if I'll be at the office before ten o'clock . . ."

He climbed the stairs with heavy steps, pondering over vague thoughts, and he found the door opened by Madame Maigret standing in her nightdress.

"Not too tired?"

"Not really . . . No . . ."

It was not weariness. He was preoccupied, uneasy, rather sad, as if the incident at Rue Notre-Dame-des-Champs had affected him personally. The doctor with the chubby face had rightly said: the Josselins were not the kind of people in whose home one would readily accept such a catastrophe.

He recalled the reactions of some of the people

31

there, of Véronique, of her husband, of Madame Josselin whom he had not yet seen and whom he had not even asked to see.

There was something disturbing about it all. He was disturbed, for example, by his own order to have Dr. Fabre's statements verified, as if the doctor were a suspect.

However, if one stuck to the facts, one was forced to consider him. The delegate of the D.A. and Gossard, the coroner, had certainly done so. If they had said nothing it was because this case gave them the same feeling of uneasiness as it did Maigret.

Who knew that the two women, mother and daughter, were at the theater that evening? Probably not many, and so far no one's name had been mentioned.

Fabre had arrived at Rue Notre-Dame-des-Champs at about half past nine. He had begun a game of chess with his father-in-law.

Someone had telephoned to tell him he had a patient to see on Rue Julie. There was nothing extraordinary about that. Probably, like all doctors, he was often inconvenienced in this way.

Nevertheless, wasn't it a disturbing coincidence that, on that particular night, the maid had not heard the name clearly? And that she had sent the doctor to an address where no one needed him?

Instead of returning to Rue Notre-Dame-des-Champs to finish the game and wait for his wife, Fabre had gone to the hospital. That, too, must happen frequently, given his personal habits.

One tenant only entered the apartment house dur-

ing that time and called out his name as he passed
the concierge's lodge. The concierge got up a little
later and stated that no one had come in or gone out
after that.

"Aren't you going to sleep?"

"Not yet . . ."

"Are you sure you want to get up at nine o'clock?"

"Yes . . ."

He took a long time to get to sleep. He kept seeing
the thin figure of the pediatrician in crumpled
clothes, his over-bright eyes those of a man who
does not get enough sleep.

Did he know he was a suspect? Had it occurred to
his wife and his mother-in-law?

Instead of telephoning the police when they discovered the body, they had first called the apartment
on Boulevard Brune. However, they were not aware
of the incident at Rue Julie. They did not know why
Fabre had left Rue Notre-Dame-des-Champs.

It had not immediately occurred to them that he
might be found at the hospital and they had turned
to the family doctor, Dr. Larue.

What had they said to each other while they waited alone in the apartment with the corpse? Was Madame Josselin already in the same state of shock?
Was it Véronique, alone, who had made the deci-
sions, while her mother remained silent and
stunned?

Larue had arrived and immediately realized the
mistake, if not the indiscretion, that they had committed by not calling the police. It was he who had
notified the police station.

All this Maigret would have liked to consider and live with by himself. It was essential to reconstruct bit by bit each moment of that night.

Who had thought of the hospital and who had lifted the receiver? Larue? Véronique?

Who had made sure that nothing had disappeared from the apartment and that it was therefore not a vicious case of burglary?

Madame Josselin was led to her bedroom. Larue stayed by her and, with Maigret's authorization, ended up by giving her a sedative.

Fabre rushed back, found the police in the home of his father-in-law, the latter dead in his armchair.

"And yet," thought Maigret as he dozed off, "it was his wife who told me about the automatic . . ."

If Véronique had not deliberately opened the drawer, knowing what she was looking for, probably no one would have suspected the existence of a weapon.

Now, didn't that eliminate the possibility of a crime committed by a stranger?

Fabre claimed to have heard his father-in-law fasten the chain across the door after having seen him out at a quarter past ten.

Josselin had therefore opened the door to his murderer himself. He had not been suspicious as he went back to his place in the chair.

If the window was open at this point, as seemed likely, someone had closed it, either Josselin or his visitor.

And if the Browning was really the murder weapon, the murderer knew of its existence in that exact place and had been able to get it without arousing suspicion.

Supposing a man came from outside, how did he get out of the building?

Maigret ended up in a restless sleep, constantly tossing and turning, and it was a relief to smell the aroma of coffee, to hear Madame Maigret's voice and see before him through the open window the roof-tops bathed in sunshine.

"It's nine o'clock . . ."

He instantly recalled the case down to the small-est detail, just as if there had been no interruption.

"Pass me the telephone directory . . ."

He looked for the Josselins' number, dialed it, lis-tened to it ring for quite awhile, then finally heard a voice he did not know.

"Is this Monsieur René Josselin's apartment?"

"He's dead."

"Who is speaking?"

"Madame Manu, the housekeeper."

"Is Madame Fabre still there?"

"Who is speaking?"

"Chief Superintendent Maigret of the Criminal Police. I was there last night . . ."

"The young lady has just left to go and change."

"And Madame Josselin?"

"She is still asleep. She was given some medicine and it looks like she won't wake up before her daughter returns."

"No one has come by?"

"Nobody. I am busy tidying up. I had no idea, when I arrived this morning . . ."

"Thank you."

Madame Maigret did not ask him any questions and he just said to her: "A decent man who got himself killed, Lord knows why . . ."

He saw Josselin in his armchair again. He endeavored to see him not dead, but alive. Had he really remained alone in front of the chessboard, and had he continued the game for awhile, sometimes moving the black pawns, sometimes the white?

If he was waiting for someone . . . knowing that his son-in-law would come and spend the evening with him, he could not have arranged a secret meeting. Or in that case . . .

One would have had to believe that the telephone call summoning Dr. Fabre to Rue Julie . . .

"It's decent people who give us the most trouble," he grumbled as he finished his breakfast and headed toward the bathroom.

He did not go directly to the Quai, but merely telephoned to make sure he was not needed.

"Rue du Saint-Gothard," he called to the taxi driver.

First he would look for information on René Josselin. Josselin certainly was the victim. But a man is not killed without reason.

There was a vacation-time air about Paris. It was no longer the empty Paris of the month of August, but a reluctance to return to the daily routine seemed to permeate the city. If it had rained, or if it had been cold it would have been easier. This year summer could not make up its mind to depart.

The taxi driver turned around as he left Rue Dareau, near the railroad embankment.

"What number?"

"I don't know. It's a cardboard factory . . ."

At another turn they saw a large concrete building with curtainless windows. Across the whole length of the façade they could read the words:

Former Owner Josselin
Successors Jouane and Goulet

"Shall I wait for you?"

"Yes."

There were two doors, one leading into the workshops and another, farther down, leading into the offices. Maigret chose the latter and found himself in an ultramodern setting.

"May I help you?"

A young girl poked her head through a window and looked at him curiously. Admittedly Maigret had that sullen expression typical of him at the beginning of an investigation; he was looking around slowly as if concentrating on taking stock of the premises.

"Who runs the firm?"

"Messrs. Jouane and Goulet" she replied, as if stating the obvious.

"I know that. But which of the two is the manager?"

"That depends. Monsieur Jouane manages mainly the artistic side and Monsieur Goulet the manufacturing and business side."

"Are they both here?"

"Monsieur Goulet is still on vacation. What do you want?"

"I want to see Monsieur Jouane."

"Who may I say is calling?"

"Chief Superintendent Maigret."

"Do you have an appointment?"

"No."

"One moment . . ."

She went off to the back of her glass-fronted cub-byhole to speak to a young girl in a white smock who, after glancing curiously at the visitor, came out of the room.

"Someone is going to get him. He's in the work-shops."

Maigret could hear the noise of the machines and, when a side door opened, he caught a glimpse of quite a large room where more young girls, more women in white, were working in rows, as if it were a chain operation.

"You asked for me?"

The man must have been about forty-five. He was tall, with an expressive face, and he, too, wore a white coverall that, unbuttoned, revealed a well-cut suit.

"If you care to follow me . . ."

They went up a light oak staircase and through a window saw half a dozen designers bent over their work. They went through one more door into a sun-ny office where a secretary was typing in a corner.

"Would you leave us, Mademoiselle Blanche."

He motioned Maigret to a seat and sat down be-hind his desk, surprised, rather concerned.

"I wonder . . ." he began.

"Have you heard about the death of Monsieur Jos-selin?"

"What did you say? Monsieur Josselin is dead? When did it happen? Was he back from his vacation?"

"You haven't seen him since his return from La Baule?"

"No. He hasn't come in to see us yet. Did he have a heart attack?"

"He was murdered."

"Monsieur Josselin?"

It was obvious that Jouane found it hard to believe.

"It's impossible. Who would have . . ."

"He was killed in his home, yesterday evening, by two gunshots . . ."

"Who did it?"

"That is what I am trying to find out, Monsieur Jouane."

"His wife wasn't with him?"

"She was at the theater with her daughter."

Jouane lowered his head, visibly shocked.

"Poor man . . . How on earth . . ."

Then indignation took over.

"But who could have . . . Listen, Superintendent . . . You didn't know him. He was the nicest man in the world . . . He has been a father to me, more than a father . . . When I started here I was sixteen and I knew nothing . . . My father had just died . . . My mother took cleaning jobs . . . I began as an errand boy, with a tricycle carrier . . . Monsieur Josselin taught me everything . . . it was he who made me a foreman later on . . . And when he decided to retire from the business he sent for us, Goulet and me . . . Goulet had started out as a machinist . . .

"He told us that his doctor had advised him to ease up on his work and that he simply could not do that . . . To come here for two or three hours a day, and just play at it, was not possible for a man like him who was used to managing everything and who stayed here working almost every night, long after the workshops closed . . ."

"Were you frightened at the thought of having a stranger for your boss?"

"I admit I was. It was a real disaster for Goulet and me and we looked at each other, in consternation, as Monsieur Josselin smiled a sly smile . . . Do you know what he did?"

"Someone told me about it last night."

"Who?"

"His doctor."

"Of course, we both had some savings, but not enough to buy a firm like this . . . Monsieur Josselin brought in his solicitor and they found a way of handing over the business to us by spacing the payments over a long period . . . A period which, needless to say, is far from over . . . In fact, for almost twenty more years . . ."

"He used to come by occasionally, even so?"

"He used to visit us discreetly, as if he was afraid of bothering us. He made sure that everything was running smoothly, that we were happy, and when we did have occasion to ask his advice he gave it as if he had no right to . . ."

"You don't know of any enemies he may have had?"

"None. He was not someone who made enemies. Everybody liked him. Go into the offices, the workshop, and ask anyone what he thought of him . . ."

"Are you married, Monsieur Jouane?"

"I am. I have three children and we live in a small home which I had built, near Versailles . . ."

He, too, was a good man! Was Maigret only going to meet "good people" on this case? He was almost irritated by it, for, after all, there was a dead man on the one hand and a man who had fired twice at René Josselin on the other.

"Did you often go to Rue Notre-Dame-des-Champs?"

"I went there four or five times in all . . . No! I'm forgetting that five years ago, when Monsieur Josselin had a bad case of flu, I stopped by every morning to give him the mail and get his orders . . ."

"Did you ever dine or have lunch there?"

"We dined there with Goulet and our wives on the evening we signed the agreement, when Monsieur Josselin handed over the business to us. . . ."

"What kind of a man is Goulet?"

"A technician, a hard worker."

"How old is he?"

"About my age. We came into the firm within a year of each other."

"Where is he now?"

"On Ile de Ré with his wife and children."

"How many children does he have?"

"Three, like me."

"What do you think of Madame Josselin?"

"I hardly know her. She seems to me to be an excellent wife. Not the same sort of person as her husband."

"How do you mean?"

"She is more stand-offish . . ."

"And their daughter?"

"She sometimes came to the office to see her father, but we had little contact with her."

"I suppose René Josselin's death does not change your financial arrangements in any way?"

"I haven't thought about that yet . . . Wait . . . No . . . There is no reason . . . Instead of paying the amounts due directly to him we will pay his heirs . . . Madame Josselin, I suppose . . ."

"Are these large amounts?"

"That depends on the years, as the arrangement allows for a share in the profits . . . But in all events there is enough on which to live very comfortably . . ."

"In your judgment, did the Josselins live very comfortably?"

"They lived well. They had a beautiful apartment, a car, a villa at La Baule . . ."

"But they could have lived in greater style?"

Jouane thought for a moment.

"Yes . . . Without a doubt . . ."

"Was Josselin miserly?"

"He would not have thought of the arrangement for Goulet and me if he had been miserly . . . No . . . Look, I think he lived as he wanted to live . . . He did not have expensive tastes . . . He preferred his peace and quiet to anything else . . ."

"And Madame Josselin?"

"She likes to look after her house, her daughter, and now her grandchildren . . ."

"How did the Josselins react to their daughter's marriage?"

"It's difficult for me to say . . . These things did not happen here but on Rue Notre-Dame-des-Champs . . . Monsieur Josselin certainly adored Mademoiselle Véronique and it must have been hard for him to be separated from her . . . I too have a daughter . . . She is twelve . . . I admit that I am dreading the moment when a stranger will take her away from me and when she will no longer even bear my name . . . I suppose all fathers feel the same way . . ."

"The fact that his son-in-law was not wealthy . . ."

"He probably would have been pleased about that . . ."

"And Madame Josselin?"

"I'm not sure . . . the idea of her daughter marrying a mailman's son . . ."

"Fabre's father is a mailman?"

"In Melun, or a village near there . . . I'll tell you what I know . . . It seems he got himself a series of scholarships . . . There is also a rumor that, if he wished, he would soon be one of the youngest professors in the Medical Faculty . . ."

"One more question, Monsieur Jouane. I am afraid it may shock you, after what you have just told me. Did Monsieur Josselin have any mistresses? Was he interested in women?"

Just as he was about to speak Maigret interrupted him.

"I presume, since you married, you have on occasion slept with a woman other than your wife?"

"Yes, I have. But I always avoided any kind of attachment. Do you understand what I mean? I wouldn't want to jeopardize the happiness of our home . . ."

"You have a lot of young women who work here . . ."

"Not them. Never. It's a matter of principle. And apart from that, it would be dangerous . . ."

"Thank you for being so frank. You consider yourself a normal man. René Josselin was a normal man, too. He married late, around the age of thirty-five . . ."

"I see what you mean . . . I'm trying to imagine Monsieur Josselin in that situation . . . I can't . . . I don't know why. I know he was like any other man, and yet . . ."

"You have never known him to have a love affair?"

"Never. Nor did I ever see him eye one of the girls who work here, although some of them are very pretty. Some must even have tried, as they have tried with me . . . No! Superintendent, I don't think you will come up with anything along those lines . . ."

He suddenly asked:

"Why hasn't this been mentioned in the papers?"

"It will be reported in this evening's papers . . ."

Maigret got up with a sigh.

44

"Thank you, Monsieur Jouane. If you think of anything else at all which might help, give me a ring . . ."

"As far as I am concerned, it is an inexplicable crime . . ."

Maigret nearly muttered crossly:

"As far as I am concerned, too."

Only he knew that inexplicable crimes do not exist. One does not kill without a very important reason.

It would not have taken much prompting for him to add:

"You don't just kill anybody."

For his experience had taught him that some people are cut out to be victims.

"Do you know when the funeral will take place?"

"The body will not be returned to the family until after the autopsy."

"That hasn't been done yet?"

"They must be doing it now."

"I must telephone Goulet immediately . . . He was not to return to work until next week . . ."

On his way out Maigret nodded to the young girl in her glass cage and wondered why she was trying not to burst out laughing as she looked at him.

3

The street was quiet, country-like, with the sun on one side and shade on the other; in the middle of the road two dogs were sniffing each other, and behind the open windows some women were getting on with their housework. Three Little Sisters of the Poor in wide skirts, the wings of their coifs fluttering like birds, were walking toward the Luxembourg Gardens. Maigret looked at them in the distance, his mind a blank. Then he frowned as he noticed a policeman in uniform grappling with half a dozen reporters and photographers outside the Josselins' apartment house.

He was used to it. It was to be expected. He had just informed Jouane that the evening newspapers would be bound to write about the case. René Josselin had been murdered and people who have been murdered are automatically public property. In a few hours a family's private life would be revealed in every detail, true or false, and everyone would have the right to express opinions.

Why did that shock him all of a sudden? It annoyed him to be shocked by it. He felt as if he was becoming caught up in the almost edifying, middle-class atmosphere which surrounded these people, "good people," as everyone kept telling him.

The photographers clicked their cameras as he got out of the taxi. The reporters surrounded him as he paid the driver.

"What do you think, Chief Superintendent?"

He brushed them aside, muttering:

"When I have something to say I will let you know. There are women in mourning up there and the decent thing would be to leave them in peace."

Now, he himself was going to disturb them. He nodded to the man in uniform, went into the building which he was seeing for the first time in daylight and which was very light and cheerful. He was about to pass by the concierge's apartment which had a white net curtain drawn across its glass door, when he changed his mind, knocked on the door, and turned the handle.

As in other buildings in fashionable districts, the concierge's apartment was a sort of small sitting room with polished furniture. A voice asked:

"Who is it?"

"Chief Superintendent Maigret."

"Come in, Chief Superintendent."

The voice came from a kitchen whose walls were painted white, where the concierge, her sleeves rolled up to the elbows and a white apron over her black dress, was busy sterilizing some bottles.

She was young and attractive, her figure still

plump from her recent pregnancy. Pointing to a door, she said in a whisper:

"Don't talk too loudly. My husband is sleeping."

Maigret remembered that her husband was a police officer and that he had been on duty the night before.

"I have been pestered by journalists since this morning and several went upstairs when my back was turned. My husband finally notified the police station and they sent over one of his colleagues . . ."

The baby was sleeping in a wicker cradle decorated with yellow ruffles.

"Have you discovered anything new?" she asked.

He shook his head.

"I presume you are sure of your facts?" he in turn asked in an undertone. "No one went out yesterday evening after Dr. Fabre had left?"

"No one, Chief Superintendent. I just told the same thing to one of your men, a large man with a red face, Inspector Torrence, I think. He spent over an hour in the building questioning the tenants. There aren't many here at the moment. Some are still on vacation. The Tuplers haven't yet returned from the United States. The building is half empty . . ."

"Have you worked here a long time?"

"Six years. I took over from an aunt of mine who spent forty years here."

"Did the Josselins entertain much?"

"Virtually never. They are quiet people, kind to everyone, and they lead a very routine life. Dr. Larue and his wife came to dinner occasionally. The Josselins went to dinner at their home, too . . ."

Like the Maigrets and the Pardons. Maigret wondered if they, likewise, had a set day.

"In the morning, at about nine o'clock, while Madame Manu was doing the housework, Monsieur Josselin would come down for his walk. This was so regular I could have set the clock when I saw him pass. He used to come into our apartment, say a few words about the weather, pick up his mail which he put in his pocket after having glanced at the envelopes, and walk slowly off toward the Luxembourg Gardens. He always walked at the same speed . . ."

"Did he get much mail?"

"Not much. Later, around ten o'clock, while he was still out, his wife in turn would come downstairs dressed to the hilt even to go shopping. I've never seen her go out without a hat."

"What time would her husband come back?"

"That depended on the weather. If it was a nice day he hardly ever came back before eleven-thirty or twelve. When it rained he didn't stay out so long but went for a stroll, even so."

"And in the afternoon?"

She had finished putting the nipples back on the bottles which she then placed in the refrigerator.

"They sometimes went out together, but not more than once or twice a week. Madame Fabre also used to come and see them. Before the birth of her second child she used to bring the oldest with her."

"Did she get on well with her mother?"

"I believe so. They used to go to the theater together, as they did last night."

"You didn't notice, these last few times, if there were any letters in the mail with an unfamiliar handwriting?"

"No."

"No one came to see Monsieur Josselin when he was alone in the apartment, for instance?"

"No. I thought about all this, last night, suspecting that you would question me. Look, Superintendent, there is nothing to report about these people . . ."

"They didn't associate with other tenants?"

"Not to my knowledge. In Paris it's rare for tenants in the same building to know each other, except in the lower-class districts. Everybody leads his own life without knowing his neighbor across the hall."

"Has Madame Fabre come back?"

"A few minutes ago . . ."

"Thank you."

The elevator stopped at the third floor, where there were two doors with a large, red-bordered mat in front of each. He rang the bell of the door on the left, and heard muffled steps. After some hesitation, the door moved and a narrow crack of bright light appeared, for the chain had not been unlatched.

"What is it?" someone asked rather crossly.

"Superintendent Maigret."

A face, with the marked features of a woman in her fifties, peered out to scrutinize the visitor with suspicion.

"Good! I believe you! There have been so many reporters this morning . . ."

The chain was slid back and Maigret saw the apartment as it usually was, with everything in its place, the sun streaming in through the two windows.

"If it's Madame Josselin you wish to see . . ."

He had been ushered into the living room, where there was now no trace of the events and confusion of the past night. A door opened immediately and Véronique, dressed in a navy-blue suit, stepped into the room.

She was obviously tired and Maigret saw on her face the same wavering, searching look. As she stared at various objects in the room or at the face of her visitor, it was as if she was seeking support or the answer to a question.

"You haven't found anything?" she murmured resignedly.

"How is your mother?"

"I have only just come in. I went to see my children and to change. I think you were told on the telephone. I don't know. I no longer know where I am. Mother did get some sleep. When she woke up she did not speak. She drank a cup of coffee but refused to eat. I wanted her to stay in bed. I haven't managed to persuade her and she is getting dressed now."

She looked around again, avoiding the armchair in which her father had died. The chessmen were no longer on the small round table. A half-smoked cigar which Maigret had noticed in an ashtray the night before had disappeared.

"Your mother hasn't said anything yet?"

"She answers me with a yes or a no. She has all her wits about her, and she appears to be thinking about

51

one thing only. Is it she you have come to see?"

"If possible . . ."

"She will be ready in a few minutes. Don't distress her too much. I ask you this favor. Everyone thinks of her as a placid woman because she is usually so self-controlled. I know, however, that she is extremely highly strung. Only she doesn't show it . . ."

"Have you often seen her very emotionally upset?"

"That depends on what you call 'very.' When I was a child, for instance, like all children I used to exasperate her. Instead of smacking me or getting angry she used to turn pale and looked as if she couldn't speak. On these occasions she nearly always shut herself up in her room and that used to make me very frightened . . ."

"And your father?"

"My father never got angry. His reaction was to smile as if he was making fun of me . . ."

"Is your husband at the hospital?"

"Since seven o'clock this morning. I left my children with the maid, as I dared not bring them with me. I don't know how we are going to cope. I don't like leaving Mother alone in the apartment. We have no guest room at home and besides, she would refuse to come . . ."

"Can't you get Madame Manu, the cleaning woman, to spend the night here?"

"She has a twenty-four-year-old grandson who is more demanding than a husband and gets angry when she has the bad luck to return home

52

late . . . We must find someone, perhaps a nurse . . . Mother will object . . . Of course, I will spend as much time as I can here . . ."

With regular features and strawberry-blond hair she was not particularly pretty, for she had no sparkle.

"I think I hear Mother . . ."

Indeed the door opened and Maigret was surprised to see before him a woman who was still very young in appearance. He knew she was fifteen years younger than her husband, but in his mind he had nevertheless expected to find a grandmother.

Now, wearing a very plain black dress, she looked more youthful than her daughter. She had brown hair and bright, almost black eyes. In spite of the tragedy, in spite of her condition, she was carefully made up and perfectly groomed.

"Superintendent Maigret . . ." he introduced himself.

Her eyelids flickered, she looked around the room and then at her daughter, who murmured immediately:

"Perhaps you would rather be alone . . . ?"

Maigret said neither yes nor no. Her mother did not stop her. Véronique left quietly. All the comings and goings in the apartment were muffled by the thick velvet-pile carpet on which old rugs lay here and there.

"Do sit down . . ." said René Josselin's widow, who remained standing by her husband's armchair.

Maigret hesitated, finally took a seat, and Madame Josselin then sat down in her own armchair near the work table. She sat up very straight, without leaning back in the chair, like women who have been brought up in a convent. Her mouth was thin, no doubt because of age, her hands slender and still beautiful.

"I apologize for disturbing you, Madame Josselin, and I must admit I don't know what questions to ask you. I can understand your confusion, your sorrow."

She looked at him with steady eyes, without flinching, causing him to wonder if she heard his words or if she was pursuing her own private monologue.

"Your husband was the victim of an apparently inexplicable crime and I am obliged not to overlook anything that might put me on the right track."

Her head moved slightly, up and down, as if she approved.

"You were at the Madeleine theater yesterday with your daughter. It is likely that whoever killed your husband knew he would find him alone. When had you decided to go out?"

She replied in a forced tone:

"Three or four days ago. I think it was Saturday or Sunday."

"Whose idea was it?"

"Mine. I was curious about this play the newspapers have talked so much about."

He was surprised, knowing in what a state she was at four in the morning, to see her answer so calmly and precisely.

"We discussed going to last night's performance with my daughter and she telephoned her husband to ask if he would come with us."

"The three of you sometimes went out together?"

"Seldom. My son-in-law is only interested in medicine and his patients."

"And your husband?"

"He and I used to go to the movies or a variety show together. He liked variety shows very much."

Her voice was toneless, with no warmth in it. She was reciting, still looking steadily at Maigret's face as one would an examiner's.

"Did you book your seats by telephone?"

"Yes. Numbers 97 and 99. I remember, because I always insist on having seats on the middle aisle."

"Who knew that you would be out that evening?"

"My husband, my son-in-law, and the housekeeper."

"No one else?"

"My hairdresser, as I went to have my hair done in the afternoon."

"Did your husband smoke?"

Maigret was jumping from one idea to another and he had just remembered the cigar in the ashtray.

"Some. A cigar after each meal. Occasionally he smoked one when he went for his morning walk."

"Forgive this silly question: you don't know of any enemies he may have had?"

She did not cry out in protest, but simply uttered: "No."

"He never gave you the impression he was hiding something, some more or less secret part of his life?"

"No."

"What did you think, last night, when you returned to find him dead?"

She seemed to swallow, and said:

"That he was dead."

Her face had become harder, even stiffer, and Maigret thought for a moment that her eyes were going to well up with tears.

"Did you not ask yourself who had killed him?"

He thought he detected an almost imperceptible hesitation.

"No."

"Why didn't you telephone the police immediately?"

She did not reply at once and looked away from the Superintendent for a moment.

"I don't know."

"You first called your son-in-law?"

"I didn't call anybody. It was Véronique who telephoned her home; she was concerned not to see her husband here."

"Wasn't she surprised not to find him at home either?"

"I don't know."

"Who thought of Dr. Larue?"

"I think I did. We needed somebody to do what had to be done."

"You haven't any suspicions, Madame Josselin?"

"None."

"Why did you get up this morning?"

"Because I had no reason to stay in bed."

"Are you sure that nothing in the house has disappeared?"

"My daughter has made sure. She knows where everything is kept just as well as I do. Apart from the gun . . ."

"When was the last time you saw it?"

"A few days ago, I can't remember exactly."

"Did you know it was loaded?"

"Yes. My husband always kept a loaded gun in the house. When we were first married he used to keep it in the drawer of his bedside table. Then, for fear Véronique might touch it, and as nothing else locks in the bedroom, he put it in the living room. For a long time that drawer was kept locked. Now that Véronique is grown-up and married . . ."

"Did your husband seem to be frightened of anything?"

"No."

"Did he keep a lot of money at home?"

"Very little. We pay for almost everything by check."

"And you never came home to find your husband with someone you did not know?"

"No."

"And you never met your husband with a stranger either?"

"No, Chief Superintendent."

"Thank you."

He was hot. He had just conducted one of the most difficult interrogations of his career. It was rather like throwing a ball that didn't bounce back. He had the impression that his questions did not touch any sore point, that they glanced off the surface, and the replies given in exchange were neutral, lifeless.

She had not eluded any of these questions, but she had not made one personal statement either.

She did not get up to show him out. She still sat just as upright in her armchair, and he could not read anything in her eyes which struck him, however, as extremely alert.

"Please forgive this intrusion."

She did not comment and waited for him to get up and walk awkwardly to the door before she rose and followed him in turn.

"If something occurs to you, if you remember or suspect anything . . ."

She replied once more by a flicker of her eyelids.

"A policeman is keeping watch at the door and I hope you will not be bothered by reporters . . ."

"Madame Manu told me they had already come . . ."

"Have you known her a long time?"

"About six months."

"Does she have a key to the apartment?"

"Yes, I had one made for her."

"Apart from her, who had a key?"

"My husband and I. Also our daughter. She has always kept the key she had when she was a young girl."

"That's all?"

"Yes. There is a fifth key which I call the emergency key and I keep it in my dressing-table."

"Is it still there?"

"I have just seen it."

"May I ask your daughter a question?"

She opened the door, disappeared for a moment, and came back with Véronique Fabre who looked from one to the other.

"Your mother tells me you kept a key to the apartment. I would like to make sure that you still have it . . ."

She walked toward a chest of drawers and picked up a blue leather handbag. She opened it and pulled out a small flat key.

"Did you have it with you yesterday at the theater?"

"No. I took an evening bag, much smaller than this one, and I put hardly anything in it."

"So that your key remained in your apartment on Boulevard Brune?"

That was all. In all decency, he saw no further questions he could ask. He was in a hurry, moreover, to get out of this cushioned atmosphere in which he felt ill at ease.

"Thank you."

He went downstairs on foot in order to stretch his legs and as he reached the first landing he let out a deep sigh. The reporters were no longer on the sidewalk, which the policeman was patrolling with long, slow strides, but at a coal merchant's across the street; they rushed up to him.

"Have you questioned the two women?"

He looked at them rather like the widow had done, as if he wasn't seeing their faces but was looking through them.

"Is it true that Madame Josselin is ill and refuses to answer questions?"

"I have nothing to say to you, gentlemen . . ."

"When do you hope . . ."

He gestured vaguely and walked toward the Boulevard Raspail to look for a taxi. As the reporters had not followed him but had taken up their watch again, he made the most of it and went into the same little café as the night before and had a short beer.

It was almost noon when he entered his office at the Quai des Orfèvres. A moment later he half-opened the door of the Inspectors' Room and saw Lapointe together with Torrence.

"Come into my office, both of you . . ."

He sat down heavily at his desk, selected his largest pipe and filled it.

"What have you been up to?" he first asked young Lapointe.

"I went to Rue Julie to do some checking. I questioned the three concierges. All three confirm that someone came, yesterday evening, to ask if there was a sick child in the building. One of them was suspicious, she thought that the man looked somewhat dubious, not like a real doctor. She came close to calling the police."

"What time was that?"

"Between half past ten and eleven . . ."

"And at the hospital?"

"That was more difficult. I arrived at a very busy time. The head physician and the doctors were making the rounds of the wards. Everybody was worn out. I saw Dr. Fabre in the distance and I am sure he recognized me."

"He didn't react?"

"No. There were several of them, in white coats, caps on their heads, following the head physician."

"Does he often call at the Children's Hospital in the evening?"

60

"Apparently they all do, either for an emergency or when they are following an important case. Dr. Fabre is the one seen there most often. I managed to catch hold of two or three nurses. They all speak of him in the same way. He's considered a sort of saint there . . ."

"Did he remain with his patient the whole time?"

"No. He went into several wards and chatted for quite awhile with a house surgeon . . ."

"Do they already know, at the hospital?"

"I don't think so. They looked daggers at me. Especially a young woman who must have been more than a nurse, an assistant I suppose, who said angrily:

" 'If you have indiscreet questions to ask, ask Dr. Fabre himself . . .' "

"The police surgeon hasn't telephoned?"

It was customary after an autopsy to give the Quai a ring since it always took some time to prepare the official report.

"He was hit by two bullets. One was lodged in the aorta and would have been enough to cause his death."

"What time does he think this happened?"

"As far as he can tell, roughly between nine and eleven o'clock. To be more precise, Dr. Ledent would like to know when Josselin had his last meal."

"You will telephone the maid for this information and relay the answer."

Meanwhile big Torrence, planted before the window, was looking at the boats on the Seine.

"What do I do next?" asked Lapointe.

61

"Get on with the telephoning first. And now, from you, Torrence . . ."

He did not use the familiar 'tu' although he had known him far longer than Lapointe. It was true that Lapointe looked more like a young student than a police inspector.

"How about these tenants?"

"I have drawn you a small plan of the building. It will be easier."

He put it on the desk, moved behind Maigret, and occasionally pointed his finger to indicate one of the squares he had drawn.

"First of all, the ground floor. You undoubtedly know that the concierge's husband is a police officer and was on night duty. He came back at seven in the morning and he did not pass the building on his beat during the night."

"Next . . ."

"On the left lives an old maid, Mademoiselle Nolan, who seems to be very rich and very tightfisted. She watched television until eleven o'clock and then went to bed. She didn't hear anything and received no visitors."

"On the right?"

"A certain Davey. He too lives alone, is a widower, and assistant manager of an insurance company. He dined in town, as he does every evening, and returned at a quarter past nine. From what I could learn, a young and rather pretty woman sometimes comes to keep him company but that was not the case yesterday. He read the papers and went to sleep about half past ten without having heard anything peculiar. It was only when the men from Forensics arrived with their equipment that he woke up. He got up and went to ask the policeman at the door what was happening."

"What was his reaction?"

"Zero. He went back to bed."

"Did he know the Josselins?"

"Only by sight. On the first floor, to the left, is the Arescos' apartment. There are six of them: all dark and overweight, the women quite pretty, and they all speak with a pronounced accent. There's the father, the mother, a sister-in-law, a tall girl of twenty, and two or three children. None of them went out last night."

"Are you sure? The concierge says . . ."

"I know. She told me too. Someone came back, shortly after the doctor left, and as he passed the concierge's apartment called out the name Aresco. . . . Monsieur Aresco is quite indignant about it. The family played cards and swears that no one left the apartment . . ."

"What does the concierge say?"

"That she is almost certain that was the name called out, and she even thought she recognized the accent."

"*Almost certain . . .*" repeated Maigret. "*She thought she recognized . . .* What do the Arescos do?"

"They have extensive business interests in South America and live there part of the year. They also own a house in Switzerland. They were there two weeks ago."

"Do they know the Josselins?"

"They claim they didn't even know their name."

"Go on."

"On the right, across the hall, is an art critic, Joseph Mérillon, at present on a government job in Athens."

"On the second floor?"

"The whole floor is occupied by the Tuplers, who are traveling in the United States."

"No servants?"

"The apartment is shut up for three months. The carpets have been sent to the cleaners."

"The third floor?"

"No one, that night, next to the Josselins. The Delilles, an elderly couple with married children, are staying on the Riviera until the beginning of October. Everyone in the building takes long vacations, Chief . . ."

"Fourth?"

"Above the Josselins are the Meurats: an architect, his wife, and their twelve-year-old daughter. They did not go out either. The architect worked until midnight and heard nothing. His window was open. Across the hall, a manufacturer and his wife, the Blanchons, who left that very day to go hunting in Sologne. On the fifth floor, yet another single woman, Madame Schwartz, who quite often invites a woman friend over in the evenings but she had no one in yesterday and went to bed early. Finally, a young couple, married last month, who are staying in Nièvre with the woman's parents. On the sixth there are just the maids' rooms . . ."

Maigret looked at the plan, disheartened. It was

true that some of the squares were empty, being apartments of people who were still at the beach, in the country, or abroad.

Nonetheless, half the building had been occupied the night before. Some tenants had been playing cards, some had been watching television, reading, or sleeping. One of them had still been working. The concierge had not been fully asleep after Dr. Fabre had left.

However, there had been two gunshots, a man had been killed in one of the squares without causing a ruffle in the daily routine of the others.

"Good people . . ."

All those others, too, were probably good people, respected, and living comfortable, transparent lives.

Had the concierge, after having opened the door for Dr. Fabre, dozed off more soundly than she thought? She was sincere, without a doubt. She was an intelligent woman who was well aware of the importance of her statement.

She claimed that someone had entered the house between half past ten and eleven and had called out the name Aresco as he passed her apartment.

Now, the Arescos swore that no one had left their apartment or returned to it that evening. They did not know the Josselins. It was plausible. No one in the building, as so often happens in Paris, particularly among the well-to-do, bothered about their neighbors.

"I wonder why a tenant, coming home, would have given the name of another tenant . . ."

"And what if it wasn't someone from the building?"

"According to the concierge, he could not have left the building without being seen . . ."

Maigret frowned.

"It seems ridiculous," he grumbled. "However, logically it's the only possible explanation . . ."

"That he may have stayed in the building?"

"At any rate until morning. . . . By day it must be easy to come and go without being noticed . . ."

"You mean to say that the murderer might have been a couple of steps away from the police, while the D.A.'s office was carrying out its search and the men from Forensics were working in the apartment?"

"There are empty rooms . . . Go and take a locksmith with you and make sure no lock has been forced . . ."

"I suppose I don't go inside the apartments?"

"Just check the locks from the outside."

"Is that all?"

"For the time being. What else can we do?"

Big Torrence looked thoughtful and concluded:

"That's right."

A crime had certainly been committed, since a man had been killed. Only it was not an ordinary crime because the victim was not an ordinary victim.

"A good man!" Maigret repeated almost angrily.

Who could have had a reason for killing that good man?

Much more of this and he would have begun to hate good people.

4

Maigret went home for lunch, which he had in front of the open window, and he noticed something his wife did every day. She used to take off her apron before sitting down at the table and often immediately afterward would fluff up her hair.

They, too, could have a maid. It was Madame Maigret who had never wanted one, claiming that if she didn't have the housework to do she would feel useless. She only agreed to a cleaning woman on certain days for the heavy work, and even then she used to redo the work after her.

Was it the same with Madame Josselin? Probably not exactly. She was meticulous, the appearance of the apartment was proof of this, but she did not feel the need, like Madame Maigret, to do everything herself.

Why, as he ate, did he begin to compare the two women who really had nothing in common?

On Rue Notre-Dame-des-Champs, Madame Josselin and her daughter were probably eating by themselves and Maigret imagined they must be observing each other furtively. Surely they were in the midst of discussing practical details.

On Boulevard Brune, Dr. Fabre, if he had come home, which was likely, was alone with his children. There was only a young maid to look after them and to do the housework. Having barely finished his meal he would go into his office where the endless procession of young children and worried mothers would continue all afternoon. Had he found someone to stay on Rue Notre-Dame-des-Champs with his mother-in-law? Would she accept the presence of a stranger?

Maigret caught himself pondering over these details as if they concerned people in his own family. René Josselin had died, and it wasn't just a matter of tracking down the murderer. Those who remained gradually had to reorganize their lives.

He would have liked to go to Boulevard Brune to get some sort of feel of the setting in which Fabre lived with his wife and children. He had been told that they lived in one of the new apartment houses near the Cité Universitaire and he visualized one of those nondescript buildings which he had seen in passing and which he readily would have called a cage. A bare, white façade, already dirty, rows of identical windows, and from top to bottom the same size rooms, bathrooms, one on top of the other and kitchens too, and paper-thin walls through which every sound could be heard.

He would have sworn that here was none of the rather ostentatious neatness of Rue Notre-Dame-

68

des-Champs, that the daily routine was not so regular, mealtimes somewhat haphazard, and that this corresponded as much with Fabre's nature as with his wife's carelessness or perhaps her inefficiency.

She had been a spoiled child. Her mother still came to see her almost every day, looked after the children, took the oldest for a walk. And she might also try to put a little order into a life that she must regard as too Bohemian.

Did the two women having lunch together realize that logically the only suspect, at this stage of the investigation, was Paul Fabre? He was the last person known to have been alone with Josselin.

Admittedly he himself could not have made the call summoning him to Rue Julie, but there were enough people devoted to him at the Children's Hospital, among others, to make it for him. He knew where the gun was kept.

And, strictly speaking, he had a motive. Of course money did not interest him. Without his father-in-law he would never have been hampered by private patients and could have devoted all his time to the hospital where he was obviously more at home than anywhere else.

But what about Véronique? Wasn't she beginning to regret having married a man whom everyone thought of as a saint? Didn't she have the urge to lead a different kind of life? With her temperament, wasn't she feeling the effects of her present home life?

After Josselin's death, the Fabres would undoubtedly receive their share of the inheritance.

Maigret tried to imagine the scene: the two men facing each other over the chessboard, silent and serious like all chess players; the doctor at some point getting up and going over to the chest were the gun was kept . . .

Maigret shook his head. It did not add up. He could not see Fabre turning around and facing his father-in-law with his finger on the trigger . . .

An argument, a discussion that turned sour and made them both insanely angry?

He tried in vain, but could not believe it. It was not in keeping with the character of the two men.

And besides, wasn't there the mysterious visitor the concierge spoke of, who had called out the name Aresco?

"Francine Pardon phoned . . . " said Madame Maigret all of a sudden, perhaps on purpose, to change his train of thought.

He was so far away in his thoughts that at first he looked at her as though her words didn't register.

"They came back from Italy on Monday. Do you remember how excited they were about their vacation together?"

This was the first vacation the Pardons had taken by themselves in over twenty years. They had gone by car, intending to visit Florence, Rome, and Naples, and to come back via Venice and Milan, stopping wherever they pleased.

"Anyway, they've asked us to dinner next Wednesday."

"Why not?"

Had it not become a tradition? They should have

had dinner with them on the first Wednesday of the month but because of vacation it had been put off.

"Apparently the trip was exhausting. There was almost as much traffic on the roads as on the Champs-Elysées and they had to spend an hour or so every evening looking for a hotel room."

"How is their daughter?"

"Fine. The baby is gorgeous . . ."

Madame Pardon, too, used to spend almost every afternoon with her daughter who had married the year before and had a baby a few months old.

If the Maigrets had had a child it would probably be married by now and Madame Maigret, like the others . . .

"Do you know what they have decided?"

"No."

"To buy a small house, by the sea or in the country, so that they can spend their vacations with their daughter, son-in-law, and the child . . ."

The Josselins had a villa, in La Baule. They all lived there together one month a year, or perhaps longer. René Josselin had retired.

This suddenly struck Maigret. The cardboard-box manufacturer had been an active man all his life, spending the best part of his time at Rue du Saint-Gothard, often returning there to work in the evening.

He saw his wife only at meal-times and during part of the evening.

Because a sudden heart attack had frightened him he had given up his business, virtually overnight.

What should he, Maigret, do if, forced to retire, he

71

found himself in the apartment with his wife all day long? It was all arranged, since they would go to live in the country and they had already bought their house.

But what if he had to stay in Paris?

Every morning Josselin left his apartment at virtually the same time, about nine o'clock, just as if leaving for his office. According to the concierge he used to walk to the Luxembourg Gardens with the slow, hesitant step of a cardiac or of people who think they might have an attack.

The Josselins did not have a dog and that surprised the Superintendent. He could easily have visualized René Josselin taking his dog for a walk. There was no cat in the apartment either.

He bought the newspapers. Did he sit down on a bench in the Gardens to read them? Did he not sometimes engage in conversation with one of his neighbors? Did he not usually meet the same person regularly, man or woman?

Just to be sure, Maigret had instructed Lapointe to go to Rue Notre-Dame-des-Champs to ask for a photograph, and by questioning the shopkeepers and the attendants in the Luxembourg Gardens to try and reconstruct the actions and morning activities of the victim.

Would that produce any results? He preferred not to think about it. This dead man whom he had never seen alive, this family whom he had never heard of the day before, had come to obsess him.

"Will you be back for dinner?"

"Yes. I hope so."

He went down to wait for the bus at the corner of

Boulevard Richard-Lenoir, stayed on the platform to smoke his pipe, looking around him at these men and women getting on with their day as if the Josselins did not exist and as if there was not a man in Paris who, goodness knows why, had killed another man.

Once in his office he got down to some irksome paper work, purposely to stop himself thinking about the case; and he must have succeeded, for at about three o'clock he was surprised, on picking up the telephone which had just rung, to hear Torrence's excited voice.

"I'm still in the area, Chief . . ."

He nearly asked:

"What area?"

"I thought it wiser to telephone you rather than come to the Quai since it's possible you might decide to come yourself . . . I've discovered something new . . ."

"Are the two women still in their apartment?"

"The three of them; Madame Manu is there too."

"What's happened?"

"We examined all the doors with a locksmith, including the ones that open onto the backstairs. None seems to have been forced. We didn't stop at the fifth floor. We went up to the sixth floor where the maids' rooms are."

"What did you find?"

"Hang on. Most were locked. As we were bending over one of the locks the door next to us half opened and we were rather taken aback to see in front of us a young girl stark naked who, not at all embarrassed, began to look curiously at us. A beautiful girl, what's more, very dark, with enormous eyes, and very Spanish or South-American looking."

Maigret waited, automatically drawing the bust of a woman on his writing pad.

"I asked her what she was doing there and she replied in bad French that this was her free time and that she was the Arescos' maid.

"'Why are you trying to open that door?' she asked suspiciously.

"She added, without appearing upset at the thought:

"'Are you burglars?'

"I explained who we were. She did not know that one of the tenants had been killed during the night.

"'That nice, large man who always smiled at me on the stairs?'

"Then she said:

"'It's not their new maid, at any rate?'

"I didn't understand. We must have looked ridiculous and I felt like asking her to put some clothes on.

"'What new maid?'

"'They must have a new maid because I heard noises in her room last night . . .'"

All at once Maigret stopped scribbling. He was furious at not having thought of this. Actually, he had begun to think about it, the previous night. There had been a moment when an idea had begun to form in his mind and he had felt himself on the brink of a discovery, as he had told Lapointe. Then someone, Saint-Hubert or the coroner, had spoken to him and consequently he had lost his train of thought.

The concierge claimed that a stranger had entered the building shortly after Dr. Fabre had left. He had given the name of Aresco, whereas the Arescos claimed that they had had no visitors and that none of the family had gone out.

Maigret had had the tenants questioned, but he had overlooked one part of the building—the maids' floor.

"Do you see, Chief? . . . Wait! . . . That's not all . . . That lock had not been forced either. . . . So I went down the backstairs to the third floor and asked Madame Manu if she had the key to the maid's room. She reached up toward a nail hooked to the right of a dresser, then looked at the wall and the nail in astonishment.

" 'Well, I never! It's not there any more . . .'

"She explained that the key to the sixth floor was always hung on this nail.

" 'Was it still there yesterday?' I insisted.

" 'I couldn't swear to it, but I am almost certain . . . I've only been up once with Madame, when I first came here, to clean the room, take away the sheets and blankets, and stick some paper around the window to keep the dust out.' "

Once on the scent it was just like Torrence to follow it with the tenacity of a bloodhound.

"I went back up to the sixth floor, where my locksmith was waiting. The young Spanish girl, who is called Dolores and whose free time must have been over, had gone downstairs again.

"It was just a common type of lock. My friend opened it easily."

"You did not ask Madame Josselin's permission?"

"No. I didn't see her. You advised me not to bother her except only if absolutely necessary. So, we

75

didn't need her. Well, Chief, we have a start! Someone spent at least part of the night in the maid's
room. The papers around the window were torn, and
the window open. It was still open when we went in.
What's more, a man had obviously been sleeping on
the mattress with his head on the bolster. Lastly,
there were cigarette butts on the floor. I say it was a
man because there was no lipstick on the butts.

"I'm calling from a bar called the Clairon, on Rue
Vavin. I thought you would like to see . . ."

"I'm on my way!"

Maigret was relieved not to have to think about
Dr. Fabre any more. Apparently everything had
changed. The concierge had not been mistaken.
Somebody had come in from the outside. That
somebody, it is true, knew not only of the drawer
with the gun, but also of the existence of the maid's
room and the place of the key in the kitchen.

Thus, the night before, while the investigation
was under way on the third floor, the murderer was
probably in the building, stretched out on a mattress, smoking cigarettes and waiting for daybreak
and for the coast to be clear.

Had there been a policeman permanently at the
door ever since? Maigret did not know. That was the
local Superintendent's concern. There was one at
the door when he had returned from Rue du Saint-
Gothard, but the concierge's husband had needed
him when the building was swarming with reporters
and photographers.

Anyway, one could count on a certain amount of
coming and going in the mornings, be it only the de-
livery men. The concierge had to see to the mail, her

baby, the reporters, several of whom had got so far as the third floor.

Maigret called Forensics.

"Moers? Could you send one of your men to check for fingerprints? There may be other clues to gather. Tell him to come armed with all his equipment. . . . I'll wait for him in my office, yes . . ."

Inspector Baron knocked at the door.

"I finally managed to get hold of the ticket office of the Madeleine Theater, Chief. There were definitely two seats booked yesterday in the name of Josselin. The two seats had been occupied, he doesn't know by whom, but they were occupied the whole evening. The show was nearly sold out, and no one left the auditorium during the performance. Of course, there were intermissions."

"How many?"

"Two. The first only lasts a quarter of an hour and few people leave their seats. The second is longer, a good half-hour, because the set change is important and rather tricky."

"At what time does that occur?"

"At ten o'clock. I have the name of the couple who were sitting just behind numbers 97 and 99. They are regulars who always have the same seats, Monsieur and Madame Demaille, Rue de la Pompe, in Passy. Shall I question them?"

"You had better . . ."

He did not want to leave anything to chance now. The expert from Forensics arrived, decked out like a magazine photographer.

"Shall I take a car?"

Maigret nodded and followed him. They found

Torrence with his elbows on the table and a glass of beer in front of him, still with his locksmith who seemed highly amused by this case.

"I don't need you any more," said the Superintendent. "Thank you."

"How are you going to get in without me? I relocked the door. Your inspector told me to . . ."

"I didn't want to take any risks . . ." muttered Torrence.

Maigret, too, ordered a beer and drank it almost in one gulp.

"All three of you had better wait for me here."

He crossed the street, went into the elevator, rang the Josselins' bell. Madame Manu opened the door and, as in the morning, did not slide back the chain. She recognized him at once and showed him in.

"Which of the two ladies do you wish to see?"

"Madame Josselin. Unless she is resting."

"No. The doctor was just here and insisted that she go back to bed but she refused. She's not the sort to be in bed during the day unless she is very ill . . ."

"No one has come by?"

"Just Monsieur Jouane who only stayed a few minutes. Then your inspector, the big one who asked me for the upstairs key. I swear to you I haven't touched it. Besides, I wonder why that key stayed hanging on its nail, as the room wasn't being used any more."

"The room has never been used since you have worked for Madame Josselin?"

"What would they have done with it since there isn't another maid?"

"Madame Josselin could have put up one of their friends, an acquaintance, if only for one night?"

"If they had had a friend to stay over, I presume they would have given him Madame Fabre's room . . . I'll go and tell Madame . . ."

"What is she doing?"

"I think they are busy preparing a list of people to be notified . . ."

They were not in the living room. After a considerable wait, Maigret saw them come in together and he had the strange feeling that it was mistrust of each other that rendered them inseparable.

"I apologize for disturbing you again. I presume Madame Manu has kept you informed?"

They both looked at each other, at the same time, before saying anything; but it was Madame Josselin who spoke.

"It never occurred to me to put the key in a different place," she said, "and I had virtually forgotten about it. What does it mean? Who could have taken it? Why?"

Her gaze was steadier, more melancholy than it had been in the morning. Her hands betrayed her nervousness.

"My inspector," explained Maigret, "so as not to bother you, took it upon himself to open the door of the maid's room. Please don't blame him. All the more as in so doing he has probably given a new direction to the investigation."

He observed her closely, watching for her reactions, but nothing gave away what she might be thinking.

"I am listening."

"When did you last go up to the sixth floor?"

"Several months ago. When Madame Manu came to work for me I went up there with her, as the last maid had left everything in a mess and indescribably dirty."

"So about six months ago?"

"Yes."

"You haven't been up there since? Nor your husband, I take it?"

"He has never been up to the sixth floor in his life. What on earth would he have done up there?"

"And what about you, Madame?" he asked Madame Fabre.

"I haven't been up for years. I went up when Olga was here. She was so kind to me and I sometimes went to see her in her room. Do you remember, Mother? That is almost eight years ago . . ."

"Some paper was stuck around the windows, wasn't it?"

"Yes. To keep the dust out."

"It has been torn up and the window was found open. Someone had been lying on the bed, a man, probably, who smoked a number of cigarettes."

"Are you sure it was last night?"

"Not yet. I have come to ask your permission to go up with my men and examine the premises thoroughly."

"I don't think it is a case of my giving you permission . . ."

"Of course, if you wish to be present . . ."

She interrupted him, shaking her head.

"The last maid you had, did she have a lover?"

80

"Not to my knowledge. She was a serious-minded girl. She was engaged and only left us to get married."

He went toward the door. Why did he again have the feeling that some kind of mistrust or animosity had lately arisen between mother and daughter?

As he left the room he would have liked to know how they behaved alone together, what they said to each other. Madame Josselin had retained her composure but the Superintendent was nonetheless convinced that she had received a shock.

And yet he would have sworn that this trouble about the maid's room was not such a surprise to her as it had been to him. As for Véronique, she had turned abruptly toward her mother with a sort of questioning look in her eyes.

What had she wanted to say, when she opened her mouth?

He rejoined the three men at the Clairon and had another beer before going with them to the backstairs of the building. The locksmith opened the door. They had some difficulty getting rid of him as he tried to make himself useful so that he could stay.

"How will you relock it, without me?"

"I'll put some seals on . . ."

"You see, Chief," said Torrence, pointing to the bed, the still-open window, and five or six cigarette butts on the floor.

"What I'd like to know, before anything else, is whether these cigarettes were smoked recently."

"That's easy . . ."

81

The expert examined a butt, sniffed it, carefully undid the paper, rubbed the tobacco between his fingers.

"I'll be able to be more precise at the Laboratory. But as of now I can tell you that these cigarettes were smoked quite recently. What's more, if you sniff around you, you will notice that in spite of the open window there's still a slight smell of tobacco in the air."

The man unpacked his instruments with the slow and careful movements of all those from the Laboratory. For them there were no dead, or rather the dead had no identity, as though they were without family, without personality. A crime was just a scientific problem. They were concerned with precise details—with fingerprints, clues, traces, dust.

"It's lucky the housework hasn't been done for a long time."

And, looking at Torrence:

"Have you trampled around much in the room? Have you touched anything?"

"Nothing except one of the cigarette butts. The locksmith and I both stayed near the door."

"So much the better."

"Will you stop by my office with the results?" asked Maigret, who did not know where to stand.

"And what shall I do?" asked Torrence.

"You will go back to the Quai . . . "

"May I wait for a few minutes to find out if there are any fingerprints?"

"If you want to . . . "

Maigret went downstairs with heavy steps, and at the back door to the third floor was tempted to ring

82

the bell. He was left with a vague, unpleasant feeling after his last interview with the two women. He felt that events had not taken place as they ought to have.

Nothing, moreover, was happening normally. But can one speak of normality when it concerns people at whose home a crime has suddenly been committed? Supposing the victim had been a man like Pardon, for example . . . What would have been the reactions of Madame Pardon, her daughter and son-in-law?

He could not imagine how they would react, although he had known the Pardons for years and despite the fact that they were the Maigrets' best friends.

In those circumstances, would Madame Pardon, too, have remained stupefied, unable to speak, without trying to remain as long as possible beside her husband's body?

He had just told them that a man had taken the key to the maid's room from the kitchen and had gone off to hide upstairs for some hours, that he was doubtless still there after the police had gone in the early hours of the morning and the two women had been left alone.

Now, Madame Josselin had barely faltered. As for Véronique, she had immediately looked at her mother who had given the impression of cutting her short.

One thing was certain: the murderer had not stolen anything. And no one, at the present stage of the investigation, seemed to have a vested interest in René Josselin's death.

That death had changed nothing for Jouane and his partner. And how could one believe that Jouane, who had only been to Rue Notre-Dame-des-Champs half a dozen times, knew where the automatic and the key in the kitchen were kept, and also the room plan of the sixth floor?

Fabre had probably never been up there. And Fabre would have had no reason to hide upstairs. In any case he wasn't there, but first at the hospital and then in the apartment on the third floor where the Superintendent had questioned him.

Having reached the ground floor he suddenly walked toward the elevator, went back up to the first floor and rang the Arescos' bell. Music was coming from behind the door, voices, a real hullabaloo. When the door opened he saw two children chasing each other and a large woman in a dressing gown who was trying to catch them.

"Are you Dolores?" he asked the young girl standing before him, dressed now in a light blue uniform with a cap of the same color over her black hair.

She gave him a broad smile. Everyone seemed to be laughing and smiling in this apartment, and living from morning till night in happy chaos.

"Si, señor . . . "

"Do you speak French?"

"Si . . . "

The large woman questioned the maid in her own language, while looking Maigret up and down.

"Doesn't she understand French?"

The young girl shook her head and burst out laughing.

"Tell her that I am from the police, like the inspector you saw upstairs, and that I would like to ask you a few questions . . . "

Dolores translated, speaking with extraordinary speed, and the plump woman took one of the children by the arm, dragged him with her into a room and shut the glass door. The music kept on. The young girl stood in front of Maigret, without inviting him in. Another door half opened, revealed a man's face, dark eyes, then closed silently.

"What time did you go up to bed yesterday?"

"Perhaps half past ten . . . I didn't look . . . "

"Were you alone?"

"Si, señor . . . "

"You did not meet anyone on the stairs?"

"No one . . . "

"At what time did you hear noises in the next room?"

"At six o'clock this morning, when I got up."

"Footsteps?"

"How do you mean, footsteps?"

She did not understand the word and he imitated someone walking, which set her off laughing again.

"Si . . . Si . . ."

"You did not see the man who was walking? The door did not open?"

"Was it a man?"

"How many of you sleep on the sixth floor?"

She needed a little time to understand each sentence. One might say she translated word by word before grasping the meaning.

She showed two fingers, saying:

"Only two . . . There is the maid of the people on the fourth floor . . . "

"The Meurats?"

"I don't know . . . The Meurats, are they on the left or the right?"

"On the left."

"No, then. It's the others . . . They left with rifles . . . I saw them yesterday morning putting them in the car . . . "

"Did their maid go with them?"

"No. But she didn't come back here to sleep. She has a boyfriend."

"So that you were alone last night on the sixth floor?"

That amused her. Everything amused her. She did not realize that only a partition had separated her from a man who was almost certainly a murderer.

"All alone . . . No boyfriend . . ."

"Thank you . . ."

There were faces, dark eyes, behind the curtain of the glass door and no doubt when Maigret left more laughter would burst forth.

He stopped once more in front of the concierge's apartment. The concierge was not in. He found himself face to face with a man in suspenders who was holding the baby in his arms and who, hastening to put him into his cradle, introduced himself.

"Police Officer Bonnet . . . Come in, Chief Superintendent. My wife has gone shopping . . . She is making the most of my week on night duty."

"I wanted to tell her as I was passing by that she

86

was not mistaken. It does appear that someone entered the building yesterday evening and may not have left it during the night."

"Has he been found? Where?"

"He hasn't been found, but we picked up his traces in one of the maids' rooms. He must have left this morning while your wife was grappling with the reporters."

"Is it my wife's fault?"

"Of course not . . . "

If it weren't for the fact that most of the tenants were away on extended vacations, there would have been five or six maids on the sixth floor of the building and one of them might possibly have come across the murderer.

Maigret hesitated before crossing the road and going once more into the Clairon. He finally did so, ordering mechanically:

"A small beer."

A few minutes later, through the window, he saw Torrence come out. He had had enough of watching his colleague from the Laboratory at work, and had had the same idea as Maigret.

"Still here, Chief?"

"I've been questioning Dolores."

"Did you get anything out of her? Was she dressed, at least?"

Torrence was still very proud, very happy at his discovery. He did not seem to understand why Maigret appeared more uneasy, more depressed than he had in the morning.

"We are on to something, aren't we? You know

there are plenty of prints up there? Our colleague is thoroughly enjoying himself. If only the murderer has a criminal record . . . "

"I am almost certain he hasn't . . . " sighed Maigret as he drained his glass.

Two hours later, in fact, the head of Criminal Records gave a negative reply. The prints taken from Rue Notre-Dame-des Champs did not correspond to any file on people having been mixed up with the law.

As for Lapointe, he had spent the afternoon showing the photograph of René Josselin to some shopkeepers in the district, to the caretakers in the Luxembourg Gardens, and to habitués of the benches. Some recognized him, some did not.

"You would see him every morning, always with the same gait . . . "

"He would watch the children playing . . . "

"He settled down with his papers and began reading them, occasionally smoking a cigar . . . "

"He looked like a nice man . . . "

To be sure!

5

Had it rained a long time during the night? Maigret
had no idea, but he was pleased to find, when he
awoke, the blackish pavements still glistening in
places where real clouds were reflected in them: not
the small, puffy pink clouds of the last few days, but
clouds with dark edges, heavy with rain.

He wanted to be done with summer, with vacations, and to find everyone back to normal again. He
frowned whenever he caught sight of a young woman in the street still wearing tight-fitting slacks suit-
able for some beach, and walking nonchalantly
through the streets of Paris in sandals, with bare
sun-tanned feet.

It was Saturday. He had intended, when he woke
up, to go and see Jouane again on Rue du Saint-Gothard, without knowing exactly why. He wanted to
see them all again, not so much to ask them precise
questions as to rub elbows with them, to get a better
feel of the environment in which René Josselin had
lived.

Something, no question about it, was escaping him. It now seemed certain that the murderer had come from outside and this widened the field of possibilities. But did it widen it that much? The fact remained that the automatic had been taken from the drawer, the key from the nail in the kitchen, and the man had gone deliberately to that room on the sixth floor.

Maigret walked to his office, as he quite often did; yet today he purposely went on foot, in order to linger with his thoughts. The air was cooler. People were already looking less sun-tanned and appeared to be back to their usual routine.

He arrived at the Quai just in time for the daily briefing and, with dossier under his arm, met the other department heads in the Commissioner's office. Each informed the Commissioner of recent cases. The head of the License Bureau, for example, suggested closing down a nightclub about which he received complaints almost every day. Darrui, on the other hand, who was head of the Vice Squad, had organized a night raid on the Champs-Elysées and three or four dozen prostitutes were in custody waiting for their fate to be decided.

"And what about you, Maigret?"

"I'm embroiled in a case involving decent people . . ." He grumbled fretfully.

"No suspect?"

"Not yet. Nothing but fingerprints not on record in our files, in other words, the fingerprints of an honest man . . ."

There had been a new crime during the night, almost a downright massacre. It was Lucas, just back from vacation, who was handling it. For the moment he was still shut in his office with the murderer, trying to understand his explanations.

It had happened between two Poles, in a hovel near Porte d'Italie. A laborer who spoke bad French, rather a wretched, puny man called Stéphane, whose last name was unpronounceable, lived there, as far as one could gather, with a woman and four small children.

Lucas had seen the woman before she had been taken to the hospital and claimed she was a splendid creature.

She was not the wife of the arrested Stéphane, but of one of his countrymen, a certain Majewski, who had been a farm laborer for three years on farms in the north.

Two of the children, the two oldest, were Majewski's. Exactly what had happened between these persons three years earlier was difficult to understand.

"He gave her to me . . ." Stéphane repeated stubbornly.

Once he had asserted:

"He sold her to me . . ."

The fact remains that, three years earlier, the cunning Stéphane had taken his countryman's place in the hovel and in the bed of the beautiful woman. The real husband had left, apparently consenting to it. Two more children were born and the whole lot of them lived in one room like gypsies in their caravan.

Then, Majewski decided to come back and, while his replacement was at work, had quite simply stepped into his shoes.

What had the two men said to each other when

Stéphane returned? Lucas was trying to find out, and it was all the more difficult as his prisoner spoke French just about as well as the Spanish or South American maid whom Maigret had questioned the previous day.

Stéphane had left. He had wandered around the area for almost twenty-four hours, not sleeping, loitering in a number of bistros, and somewhere along his way he had got hold of a good butcher's knife. He claimed he did not steal it and strongly insisted on this point, as if for him it was a question of honor.

During the course of the previous night he had crept into the room where everyone was asleep and had killed the husband with four or five stabs of the knife. He had then rushed at the woman, who cried out, her breasts exposed as he had struck her two or three times, but some neighbors had rushed in before he had time to finish her off.

He had not resisted arrest. Maigret went into Lucas's office to listen to part of the interrogation. Lucas was sitting at his typewriter, slowly typing out the questions and answers.

The man, sitting on a chair, was smoking a cigarette he had just been given and there was an empty cup of coffee beside him. He had been handled somewhat roughly by his neighbors. His shirt collar was torn, his hair disheveled, and his face scratched.

He listened to Lucas speaking, eyebrows knotted, making a great effort to understand; then he pondered, slowly shaking his head in bewilderment.

"He had given her to me . . ." he repeated at last, as if that explained everything. "He had no right to take her back . . ."

It seemed to him quite natural to have killed his former friend. He would have killed the woman too, if the neighbors had not intervened in time. Would he have killed the children?

He did not reply to this question, perhaps because he did not know the answer himself. He had not thought out everything beforehand. He had decided to kill Majewski and his wife. As for the rest . . .

Maigret returned to his office. There was a note informing him that the people from Rue de la Pompe who were seated behind Madame Josselin and her daughter at the theater remembered the two women very clearly. They said both women had remained in their seats during the first intermission, had gone out during the second, returned to their seats well before the curtain went up, and had not left their seats during the performance.

"What shall I do today, Chief?" Lapointe had just asked him.

"The same as yesterday afternoon."

In other words, go over the route René Josselin took every morning on his walk and question people.

"He must have occasionally spoken to somebody. Try again, at the same time of day as he . . . Have you a second photograph? Give it to me . . ."

Maigret stuffed it into his pocket, just in case. Then he took a bus to Boulevard Montparnasse and had to put out his pipe as there was no smoking on the bus.

He needed to stay in contact with Rue Notre-Dame-des-Champs. Some, at Police Headquarters, grumbled that he was bent on doing everything himself, including tedious tailing, as though he did not trust his inspectors. They did not realize that it was essential for him to probe people's lives down to the core, to try to put himself in their shoes.

If it had not been out of the question he would have moved into the Josselins' apartment, sat himself down at the table with the two women, and perhaps might have accompanied Véronique to her home in order to sense how she behaved with her husband and her children.

He, himself, wanted to take the same daily stroll as Josselin took every morning, to see what he saw, to stop at the same benches.

Once again it was the time of day the concierge sterilized the baby's bottles and she had put on her white apron.

"They've just brought in body," she told him, visibly disturbed.

"Is the daughter upstairs?"

"She arrived about half an hour ago. Her husband brought her."

"Did he go up?"

"No. He seemed in a hurry."

"There's no one else in the apartment?"

"The undertaker's men. They've already delivered all the funeral trappings."

"Did Madame Josselin stay here alone last night?"

"No. Around eight o'clock her son-in-law arrived with an elderly lady who was carrying a small suitcase and she stayed up there after the doctor left. I suppose she's a visiting nurse or one from the hospital. Madame Manu arrived as usual at seven o'clock this morning, and she's now out doing the market-ing."

He could not remember if he had already asked the question and, even if he had, he repeated it because it bothered him.

"You haven't noticed anyone, particularly in the last few days, who seemed to be lurking around the building?"

She shook her head.

"Madame Josselin never had any visitors when her husband was out?"

"Not in the six years I've been here."

"And what about him? He was often alone in the afternoon. Nobody went up to see him? Didn't he sometimes go out for a few minutes?"

"Not as far as I know . . . I think I would have noticed if he had . . . Of course, when nothing peculiar is going on you don't think about those things . . . I didn't take any more notice of them than I did of the other tenants, rather less in fact, precisely because they were never any bother . . ."

"Do you know from which direction Monsieur Josselin used to come back?"

"It depended. I've seen him come back by way of the Luxembourg Gardens, but sometimes he used to go around by Montparnasse and Rue Vavin. He wasn't a robot, right?"

"Always by himself?"

"Always by himself."

"Dr. Larue hasn't returned?"

"He stopped by late yesterday afternoon and stayed quite a long time up there."

Yet another person Maigret would have liked to meet with again. He felt that each of them could teach him something. He did not necessarily suspect them of lying but, deliberately or not, of hiding part of the truth.

Particularly Madame Josselin. Not once had she appeared relaxed. She seemed to be on her guard, doing her best to anticipate the questions that he was going to ask, and having her answers ready.

"Thank you, Madame Bonnet. Is the baby well? Did he sleep all night?"

"He woke up only once and went right back to sleep again. It's funny that on that particular night he should have been so restless, as if he felt something was going on. . . ."

It was half past ten in the morning. Lapointe should be busy questioning the people in the Luxembourg Gardens as he showed them the photograph. They were looking carefully, solemnly shaking their heads.

Maigret decided to try Boulevard de Montparnasse himself, then perhaps Boulevard Saint Michel. To start, he went into the little bar where he had had his beers the day before.

The waiter asked at once, as if he was an old customer:

"The same?"

He said yes without thinking, although he did not really feel like a beer.

"Did you know Monsieur Josselin?"

"I didn't know his name. When I saw a picture of him in the newspaper I remembered him. He used to have a dog, an old Alsatian crippled with rheumatism who tagged along after him with his head down . . . But I'm talking about seven or eight years ago at least. I've been here for fifteen years now . . ."

"What became of the dog?"

"He must have died of old age. I think it was really the young lady's dog . . . I remember her very well too."

"You never saw Monsieur Josselin in the company of a man? You never had the impression that someone was waiting for him when he left home?"

"No . . . I knew him by sight, you know. He never came in here. One morning when I was on Boulevard Saint-Michel I saw him coming out of the betting office. That surprised me. Every Sunday I usually put my bet on the tierce, but it surprised me that a man like him should play the horses."

"You only saw him at the pari-mutuel that once?"

"Yes . . . Frankly, I am hardly ever out at that time of day . . ."

"Thank you . . ."

There was a grocery next door into which Maigret entered, the photograph in his hand.

"Do you know him?"

"Of course! It's Monsieur Josselin."

"Did he happen to come into your shop?"

"Not him. His wife. They've been customers of ours for fifteen years . . ."

"Did she always do the shopping herself?"

"She used to stop in to give her order which was delivered a little later. Sometimes it was the maid.

At one time it may have been their daughter."

"You never saw her with a man?"

"Madame Josselin?"

They looked at him in amazement and even with reproach.

"She was not the sort of woman to have clandestine meetings, certainly not in the neighborhood."

Never mind! He would continue to ask the question, just the same. He went into a butcher's shop.

"Do you know . . ."

The Josselins did not buy from that particular butcher and he answered rather curtly.

Yet another bar. He went in, and as he had started off with a beer, he asked for one and took the photograph out of his pocket.

"I think it's someone from around here . . ."

How many people were he and Lapointe each going to question like this? And yet they could only count on chance. Admittedly chance had already just played a hand. Maigret now knew that René Josselin had a passion, however tame it might be, a mania, a habit: he played the horses.

Did he play for large stakes? Or was he content with placing small bets, just for the fun of it? Did his wife know? Maigret would have sworn she did not. It did not fit with the apartment on Rue Notre-Dame-des-Champs, with the characters as he knew them.

There was therefore one slight flaw. Why should there not be others?

"Excuse me, Madame . . . Do you . . ."

The photograph, once more. A shake of the head.

He started off again farther on, went into another butcher's, this time the right one, serving Madame Josselin or Madame Manu.

"We saw him go by almost always at the same time of day . . ."

"Alone?"

"Except when he used to meet his wife on his way back from his walk."

"And was she always alone too?"

"Once she came in with a little boy, a toddler, her grandson . . ."

Maigret went into a brasserie on Boulevard de Montparnasse. It was virtually empty at that time of day. The waiter was sweeping the floor.

"A small glass of something, but not beer," he ordered.

"An aperitif? A brandy?"

"A brandy . . ."

And then, just when he least expected it, he got some results.

"Yes, I know him. I thought of him right away when I saw his picture in the newspaper. Except that lately he wasn't quite so fat."

"Did he sometimes come in here for a drink?"

"Not often . . . Perhaps five or six times, always at a time of day when there was no one here. That's what drew my attention to him."

"At about this time?"

"Roundabout now . . . Or a little later."

"Was he alone?"

"No. There was someone with him, and each time they sat right at the back of the room."

"A woman?"

"A man."

"What kind of man?"

"Well dressed, still quite young . . . I would say about forty to forty-five."

"Did they appear to be discussing something?"

"They spoke in an undertone and I didn't hear what they were saying."

"When was the last time they came?"

"Three or four days ago."

Maigret hardly dared believe it.

"Are you sure you're really talking about this person?"

He showed him the photograph again. The waiter agreed to look at it more closely.

"It's just as I told you! He even had some newspapers in his hand, three or four at least, and when he left I ran after him to give them back as he had left them behind on the seat."

"Would you recognize the man who was with him?"

"I might. He was tall, with brown hair. . . . He wore a light-colored suit, light-weight, very well cut."

"Did they seem to be quarreling?"

"No. They looked serious but they weren't quarreling."

"What did they drink?"

"The fat one, Monsieur Josselin, had a quarter bottle of Vittel and the other one had a whisky. He must be used to drinking it as he specified the brand he wanted. Since I didn't have that particular brand, he gave me the name of another."

"How long did they stay?"

"Twenty minutes? Perhaps a little longer."

"You only saw them together that once?"

"I would swear that when Monsieur Josselin came in before, several months ago, well before vacation time, he was with the same man. What's more, I saw that man again . . ."

"When?"

"On the same day . . . in the afternoon . . . or was it the following day? . . . No! It was definitely the same day."

"This week, then?"

"Definitely this week . . . On Tuesday or Wednesday."

"Did he come back alone?"

"He sat alone for quite awhile reading an evening paper. He had ordered the same kind of whisky as he had that morning. Then a lady joined him."

"Do you know her?"

"No."

"A young woman?"

"On in years—not young, not old. A real lady."

"Did they appear to know each other well?"

"Most certainly. She appeared to be in a hurry. She sat down beside him and, when I went over to take her order, she indicated that she didn't want anything."

"Did they stay very long?"

"About ten minutes. They did not leave together. The woman went out first. The man had another drink before leaving."

"Are you certain it was the same man who was with Monsieur Josselin in the morning?"

"Absolutely certain. And he drank the same brand of whisky."

"Did he give you the impression of one who drinks a lot?"

"Of someone who drinks but who can hold it. He wasn't the least bit drunk, if that's what you mean, but he had bags under his eyes . . . okay?"

"And that was the only time you saw the man and woman together?"

"The only time I remember. At certain times of the day you pay less attention. There are other waiters in the place."

Maigret paid for his drink and found himself back on the sidewalk, wondering what his next move was going to be. Tempted as he was to go directly to Rue Notre-Dame-des-Champs, he loathed the thought of arriving there when the body had only just been returned to the family and when they were busy preparing the room in which it was to be laid out.

He preferred to continue on his way to the Closerie des Lilas, still going into some shops, showing the photograph with less animation.

He thus came to know the Josselins' vegetable man, the cobbler who mended their shoes, the *patisserie* where they indulged themselves.

Then as he reached Boulevard Saint-Michel, he decided to go down it again as far as the main entrance to the Luxembourg Gardens, taking Josselin's daily walk in reverse. Opposite the gate he found the stand where Josselin used to buy his papers.

Showing the photograph. Asking questions, always the same ones. At any minute he expected to see young Lapointe, who was working from the opposite direction, appear on the scene.

"That's definitely him . . . I kept his newspapers and weeklies for him."

"Was he always alone?"

The old woman thought for a moment.

"Once or twice, I think . . ."

Once, in any case, when someone was standing by Josselin, she had asked:

"Yes, sir?"

And the man had replied:

"I am with the gentleman . . ."

He was tall and dark, as far as she could remember. When was this? In the spring, because the horse chestnuts were in bloom.

"You haven't seen him recently?"

"I haven't noticed him . . ."

It was in the bistro from which the pari-mutuel operated that Maigret rejoined Lapointe.

"Have you found out, too?" said Lapointe in amazement.

"What?"

"That he used to come here . . ."

Lapointe had had time to question the manager. The latter did not know Josselin by name but he was explicit in his description.

"He came in two or three times a week and placed a bet for 5000 francs each time . . ."

Not possible! He did not look like a racetrack man. He did not carry the racing sheets. He did not study the odds.

"There are quite a lot of people now who, like

him, don't know which stable the horse belongs to or the meaning of the word handicap. They make up numbers, like other people do for the National Lottery, and ask for a ticket ending in such and such a figure."

"Did he sometimes win?"

"Once or twice he did."

Maigret and Lapointe crossed the Luxembourg Gardens together. Some students sitting on iron chairs were immersed in their studies, one or two couples with their arms around each other were casually looking at the children playing under the watchful eyes of their mother or their nurse.

"Do you think Josselin kept things from his wife?"

"I get that impression. I'll soon know . . ."

"Are you going to question her? Shall I come with you?"

"Yes, I'd just as soon have you there."

The small van belonging to the undertaker's men was no longer at the curb. The two men took the elevator, rang the bell, and once more Madame Manu half opened the door, cautiously leaving the chain in place.

"Ah! It's you . . ."

She ushered them into the living room where nothing had been changed. The dining-room door was open and an elderly lady, sitting by the window, was busy knitting. Doubtless the nurse or hospital attendant whom Dr. Fabre had brought in.

"Madame Fabre has just returned to her home. Shall I tell Madame Josselin you are here?"

And in a whisper the housekeeper added:

"Monsieur is in here . . ."

She pointed to Véronique's old bedroom, then went to call her mistress. The latter was not in the room where the body was laid out but in her own bedroom and she appeared dressed in black as she had been the day before with gray pearls around her neck and on her ears.

She still did not look as if she had been crying. Her eyes were steady, her look just as intense.

"You wish to speak to me?"

She looked curiously at Lapointe.

"One of my inspectors . . ." murmured Maigret. "I am sorry to bother you again . . ."

She did not ask them to sit down, as though she assumed their visit would be a brief one. She did not ask any questions, but waited, her eyes fixed on the Superintendent's.

"No doubt my question will seem ridiculous, but I would like to ask you first of all if your husband was a gambler."

She did not start. Maigret even had the impression that she experienced a certain relief and her lips relaxed slightly to utter:

"He played chess, most of the time with our son-in-law, sometimes but not very often with Dr. Larue . . ."

"He didn't speculate in the Stock Exchange?"

"Never. He had a horror of speculative investment. Some years ago it was proposed that his business should become a stock company in order to give him more range, and he indignantly refused."

"Did he buy any National Lottery tickets?"

"I have never seen any in the house . . ."

"He didn't bet on horses either?"

"I don't think we went to Longchamp or Auteuil more than ten times in our life, just to have a look. Once, a long time ago, he took me to see the prix de Diane at Chantilly and he never went near the betting windows."

"He could have bet at the pari-mutuel?"

"What is that?"

"In Paris and in the provinces there are offices, mostly in cafés or bars, where bets are taken . . ."

"My husband was not a café habitué."

There was a note of scorn in her voice.

"I take it you do not go to them either?"

Her face tightened and Maigret wondered if she might lose her temper.

"Why do you ask me that?"

He hesitated to urge this line of questioning right now, wondering whether it was to his advantage, from now on, to arouse her suspicions. An awkward silence established itself among the three figures. The nurse or attendant had tactfully got up and closed the dining-room door.

Behind another door there was a dead man, black drapes, and no doubt lighted candles and a sprig of boxwood dipped in holy water.

The woman in front of Maigret was the widow, he could not forget that. She was at the theater with her daughter when her husband had been killed.

"May I ask you if, this week, on Tuesday or Wednesday, you did not happen to go into a café . . . A café in the neighborhood . . ."

"My daughter and I went for a drink when we left the theater. My daughter was very thirsty. We did not stay long . . ."

"Where was that?"

"On Rue Royale."

"I'm talking about a brasserie in the neighborhood, on Tuesday or Wednesday . . ."

"I don't see what you mean . . ."

Maigret was embarrassed by the role he was obliged to play. He felt, yet without being sure, that the blow had struck home and that she needed all her strength in order not to reveal her panic.

It had lasted only a fraction of a second and she had not looked away from him.

"Someone, for whatever reason, could have arranged to meet you not far from here, on Boulevard de Montparnasse for example . . ."

"No one arranged to meet me . . ."

"May I ask you to let me have one of your photographs?"

She nearly said:

"What for?"

She controlled herself, merely muttering:

"I suppose I have no choice but to obey . . ."

It was a little as if the hostilities had just begun. She left the room, went into her bedroom whose door she left open, and one could hear her rummaging through a drawer which must have been full of papers.

When she came back she held out a passport photograph, four or five years old.

"I presume this will do?"

Maigret, taking his time, slipped it into his wallet.

"Your husband played the horses," he stated at the same time.

"In that case, I did not know about it. Is that forbidden?"

"It is not forbidden, Madame, but if we are to have a chance of finding his murderer we need to know everything. I did not know this house three days ago. I knew neither about your life, nor about your husband's. I have asked for your cooperation . . ."

"I have answered you."

"I would like you to have told me more . . ."

Since war was declared, he went into the attack.

"I did not insist upon seeing you on the night of the tragedy, as Dr. Larue maintained that you were in a severe state of shock. Yesterday I came . . ."

"I received you."

"And what did you tell me?"

"What I was able to tell you."

"Which means?"

"What I knew."

"Are you sure you have told me everything? Are you certain that your daughter or your son-in-law may not be hiding something from me?"

"Are you accusing us of lying?"

Her lips were trembling slightly. No doubt she was making an enormous effort to remain collected and dignified, facing Maigret, who looked rather flushed. And Lapointe, embarrassed, did not know where to look.

"Perhaps not of lying, but of omitting certain things. For instance I know for a fact that your husband gambled at the pari-mutuel . . ."

"And how does that help you?"

"If you knew nothing about it, if you never suspected it, it shows that he was capable of hiding something from you. And, if he hid that from you . . ."

"Perhaps he did not think of telling me."

"That would be plausible if he had gambled once or twice, by chance; but he did so regularly and laid on several thousand francs a week on bets . . ."

"What are you driving at?"

"You had given me the impression, and you have continued to do so, that you knew everything about him and that you, likewise, hid nothing from him . . ."

"I do not understand what this has to do with . . ."

"Let us suppose that on Tuesday or Wednesday morning he had an appointment with someone in a brasserie on Boulevard Montparnasse . . ."

"Was he seen there?"

"There is at least one witness to confirm this."

"It could be that he met an old friend, or a former employee and invited him for a drink . . ."

"You stated positively that he did not frequent cafés . . ."

"I do not mean that on an occasion like that . . ."

"He didn't speak to you about it?"

"No."

"He did not say, when he came back: 'By the way, I met So and So . . .'"

"I don't remember."

"If he had done so, you would remember?"

"Probably."

"And if you, likewise, had met a man whom you knew well enough to join in a café for ten minutes or so while he had a whisky . . ."

Sweat stood in droplets on his forehead and he fiddled crossly with his pipe that had gone out.

"I still don't understand."

"I am sorry to have disturbed you . . . I will no doubt have to come back. Meanwhile I ask you to think seriously . . . Someone killed your husband and is, at this moment, free . . . Perhaps he will kill again."

She was very pale, but she still did not falter and began to walk toward the door. She said good-by with just a brisk nod of the head, then closed the door behind them.

In the elevator, Maigret mopped his brow with his handkerchief. He appeared to avoid Lapointe's eyes, as though he were afraid he might see a look of reproach in them, and muttered:

"I had to . . ."

6

The two men stood on the sidewalk, close by the building, like people who are reluctant to part company. A very fine rain, barely visible, had begun to fall, tinkling bells began to ring at the bottom of the street, to which others replied in a different direction, and then in yet another.

A short distance from Montparnasse and its night-clubs, running along the Luxembourg Gardens there was not only a pleasant middle-class block of houses, but a virtual gathering of convents. Behind the Little Sisters of the Poor were the Servants of Mary; nearby, on Rue Vavin, the Ladies of Sion and, in the other part, on Rue Notre-Dame-des-Champs, yet another, the Ladies of St. Augustine.

Maigret seemed to be listening to the sound of the bells, breathed in the air mingled with invisible drops of rain, and then, after heaving a sigh, said to Lapointe:

"I want you to go over to Rue du Saint-Gothard. You'll be there in a few minutes by taxi. On a Saturday the offices and workshops will probably be closed. Even so, if Jouane is anything like his former boss there's a good chance he'll have gone back to finish some pressing work. If not, you're bound to find a concierge or a caretaker. If need be ask for Jouane's home telephone number and call him.

"I want you to bring back a framed photograph that I saw in his office. While he was talking to me yesterday I looked at it mechanically, not suspecting that it could prove useful. It's a group photograph, with René Josselin in the middle, Jouane and probably Goulet to his left and right, other members of the firm, both men and women, in rows behind them, about thirty people in all.

"None of the girls are there; just the oldest or most important employees. I suppose the photo was taken on some anniversary or else when Josselin left the firm."

"Shall I meet you back at the office?"

"No. Come and meet me at the brasserie on Boulevard Montparnasse, where I was just a while ago."

"Which one is that?"

"I believe it's called the brasserie Franco-Italienne. It's next to an art supply store."

He went on his way, hunched over, puffing at the pipe he had just lit and which, for the first time that year, had a taste of autumn about it.

He still felt somewhat uneasy about his harshness with Madame Josselin and realized that far from having got this behind him it was only just beginning. She was probably not the only one who was hiding something from him or lying. And it was his job to discover the truth.

Maigret always found it distressing to force someone into a corner, and this went back a long way, to his early childhood and his first year at school in the village of Allier.

He had, at that time, told the first big lie of his life. The school handed out textbooks which had served their purpose and were rather faded and worn, but some of the pupils got nice new books which made him envious.

He had been given, among others, a Catechism with a greenish cover, its pages already yellow, while some of his more fortunate friends had bought themselves new ones, a new edition with an attractive pink binding.

"I've lost my Catechism," he had announced to his father one evening. "I told the teacher and he has given me a new one . . ."

Now, he had not lost it. He had hidden it in the attic, not daring to destroy it.

He had had a hard time getting to sleep that night. He felt guilty and was convinced that one day his trick would be discovered. The next day he found no pleasure at all in using his new Catechism.

For three days, perhaps four, he suffered like that, until he had finally gone to the teacher with the book in his hand.

"I've found the old one," he had stammered out, red-faced and with a dry throat. "My father told me to return this one . . ."

He still remembered the look the teacher gave

113

him, a look which was both knowing and kind. He was sure the man had guessed, had understood everything.

"Are you pleased you found it?"

"Oh, yes, sir . . ."

All his life he had remained grateful to him for not having forced him to admit his lie and for having spared him humiliation.

Madame Josselin was also lying, and she was no longer a child; she was a woman, a mother, a widow. He had, as it were, forced her to lie. And others around her were probably lying for one reason or another.

He would have liked to lend them a helping hand, to spare them that terrible ordeal of fighting against the truth. They were good people: he was willing to believe this, and he was even convinced of it. Neither Madame Josselin, nor Véronique, nor Fabre were killers.

Nonetheless, all three were hiding something which would probably have enabled him to put his hands on the murderer.

He glanced at the houses opposite, thinking that it would perhaps be necessary to question one by one all the inhabitants of that street, all those who might have come upon some interesting bit of information by looking out their windows.

Josselin had met a man, either the day before his death or on the day he died, the waiter in the café could not say precisely which. Maigret was going to find out if it was, indeed, Madame Josselin who had joined that same man in the afternoon in the quiet of a café.

He arrived at the brasserie a little while later and the atmosphere was somewhat changed. People were drinking apéritifs and a row of tables had already been set for lunch.

Maigret sat down at the same place as in the morning. The waiter who had served him came up as if he was already an old customer and the Superintendent pulled the passport photograph from his wallet.

"Do you think that's she?"

The waiter put on his glasses and examined the small square photograph.

"She's not wearing a hat, here, but I'm almost sure that it's the same woman . . ."

"Almost?"

"I'm certain of it. Only if I have to testify in court one day, with judges and lawyers asking me a whole lot of questions . . ."

"I don't think you will have to testify."

"I'm positive it's she, or else someone very much like her . . . She was wearing a dark wool dress, not completely black, it had small gray flecks in the wool, and a hat trimmed with white . . ."

The description of the dress corresponded to the one Madame Josselin had been wearing that very morning.

"What can I get you?"

"A brandy and water . . . Where's the telephone?"

"In the back, on the left, opposite the washroom. Ask for a token at the counter."

Maigret shut himself in the booth and looked up Dr. Larue's number. He was not too sure of finding him at home. He had no precise reason for calling the doctor.

He was clearing the ground, as he had done with the photograph from Rue du Saint-Gothard. He was trying to eliminate even the wildest of suppositions.

A man's voice answered.

"Is that you, Doctor? This is Maigret."

"I have just come in and I was thinking of you, in fact."

"Why?"

"I don't know. I was thinking about your investigation, about your job. . . . It's a stroke of luck you found me in at this time of day. On Saturdays I finish my rounds earlier than on other days as most of my patients are out of town."

"Would you mind coming and having a drink with me at the brasserie Franco-Italienne?"

"I know the place . . . I'll be right over. Are you on to something new?"

"I don't know yet . . ."

Larue, small, chubby, and balding, did not match the description the waiter had given of Josselin's companion. Nor did Jouane, who had reddish hair and did not look as if he were a drinker.

Maigret was nevertheless determined not to let any chance slip by. A few minutes later the doctor got out of his car, joined Maigret, and spoke to the waiter as if he were on familiar ground:

"How are you, Emile? And how are those scars?"

"You can hardly see anything now . . . A glass of port, Doctor?"

They knew each other. Larue explained that he

had treated Emile a few months earlier, when the latter had scalded himself with the percolator.

"Another time, a good ten years ago, he cut himself with a chopping-knife. . . . And your investigation, Superintendent?"

"I'm not getting much help," said the latter bitterly.

"Are you speaking of the family?"

"Of Madame Josselin in particular. I would like to ask you two or three questions about her. I already asked you some the other evening. There are some things that are bothering me. If I understand correctly, you and your wife were virtually the only close friends of the family . . ."

"That's not quite right. As I told you, I have been looking after the Josselins for a long time and I have known Véronique ever since she was a little girl. But at that time I was called only occasionally . . ."

"When did you start to become a friend of the family?"

"Much later. Once, some years ago, we were invited to dinner together with some other people, the Anselmes who are large chocolate manufacturers, I still remember . . . You must know Anselme chocolates. They also make the sugared almonds for christenings."

"Did they seem to be close to the Josselins?"

"They were on quite friendly terms. They're a somewhat older couple. Josselin supplied Anselme with the boxes for the chocolates and sugared almonds."

"Are they in Paris now?"

"That would surprise me. Old Anselme retired four or five years ago and bought a villa in Monaco. They live there all year round."

"I want you to try and recall. Whom else did you meet at the Josselins?"

"More recently, I happened to spend the evening at Rue Notre-Dame-des-Champs with the Mornets who have two daughters and are on a cruise in the Bermudas at the moment. They are in the paper business. The Josselins associated with hardly anyone except a few important clients and some suppliers . . ."

"You don't remember a man approximately in his forties?"

"I can't recall, no . . ."

"You are well acquainted with Madame Josselin. What do you know about her?"

"She is a highly nervous woman and I won't conceal the fact that I prescribe tranquilizers for her; still, she is quite extraordinarily controlled."

"Did she love her husband?"

"I am convinced she did. . . . She must have had an unhappy childhood, as far as I've been able to gather. Her father lost his wife early in the marriage and was an embittered man and excessively strict."

"They lived near Rue du Saint-Gothard?"

"Close by, on Rue Dareau. She got to know Josselin and they married after a year's engagement."

"What became of the father?"

"He was stricken with a particularly painful cancer and committed suicide a few years later."

"What would you say if someone told you that Madame Josselin had a lover?"

118

"I would not believe it. You see, in my profession I share the secrets of many families. The number of women, especially women of a certain milieu, the milieu the Josselins' belong to, who have extramarital affairs is much smaller than you would think from the novels we read or the plays we see.

"I don't mean that this is always due to chastity. Perhaps lack of opportunity, or fear for their reputation has something to do with it. . . ."

"She often used to go out alone in the afternoons."

"Like my wife, like most wives. That doesn't mean to say they are going off to meet a man in a hotel or in what years ago used to be called a bachelor flat. . . . No, Superintendent, if you are asking me that question in all seriousness, I am answering you with a categorical No. You are on the wrong track there. . . ."

"And Véronique?"

"I am tempted to tell you the same thing but I would rather reserve my opinion. . . . It's unlikely. It's not altogether impossible. Chances are that she had some experiences before she married. She was studying at the Sorbonne. She met her husband in the Latin Quarter and must have known other men before him. She may be somewhat disappointed with the life he has her lead . . . I wouldn't swear to it. . . . She thought she was marrying a man, and she married a doctor. . . . Do you see what I mean?"

"Indeed."

He was making no progress—getting nowhere. He felt as if he were floundering and sullenly drank his brandy.

"Someone killed René Josselin . . ." he sighed.

Up to now this was the only certainty. And also that a man, about whom nothing was known, had met the box manufacturer as if in secret, in this same brasserie, and afterwards had met with Madame Josselin.

In other words, the husband and wife had been hiding something from each other. Something connected with one and the same person.

"I can't think who it could be . . . I'm sorry I can't be more of a help to you. . . . Now, it's time I got back to my wife and children . . ."

Besides, Lapointe now came into the café, a flat package under his arm, and looked around for Maigret.

"Was Jouane in his office?"

"No. He wasn't at home either. They've gone to spend the weekend in the country with a sister-in-law. I promised the caretaker I'd bring the photograph back today for sure and he didn't make too much of a fuss."

Maigret called the waiter, unwrapped the package.

"Do you recognize anyone?"

The waiter put his glasses back on and looked at the row of faces.

"Monsieur Josselin, of course, in the middle . . . he's a little fatter in the photograph than the man who came in the other day, but it's definitely him . . ."

"And the others? The people on the right and left?"

Emile shook his head.

"No. I've never seen them. He's the only one I recognize."

"What will you have to drink?" Maigret asked Lapointe.

"Anything."

He was looking at the doctor's glass which still held some reddish liquid.

"Is that port? The same for me, waiter."

"And you, Superintendent?"

"No more, thank you . . . I think we'll have a bite to eat here."

He did not feel like going back to Boulevard Richard-Lenoir for lunch. A little later they went over to the other side of the café, where meals were being served.

"We'll get nothing out of her," grumbled Maigret, who had ordered sauerkraut. "Even if I summon her to the Quai and question her for hours, she won't talk . . ."

He resented Madame Josselin and yet at the same time he pitied her. She had just lost her husband under tragic circumstances—her whole life was shattered. Overnight she had become a woman alone in an apartment that now was too big for her. And the police were pursuing her unrelentingly.

What secret had she decided to protect at all costs? Everyone has the right to his private life, to his secrets, hasn't he, up to the day tragedy strikes and society begins to demand some explanations.

"What are you going to do, Chief?"

"I have no idea. . . . Find this man, of course. It's not as if he were a thief. If he's the one who murdered Josselin that evening he must have had, or thought he had, very good reasons . . .

"The concierge hasn't a clue. In the six years she's been there she has never noticed a somewhat suspicious visitor. It may go back further in the past . . .

"I can't remember where she told me her aunt, the previous concierge, had gone to live when she retired . . . I'd like you to ask her, then find this woman and question her . . ."

"And what if she lives devil knows where in the province?"

"It might well be worth going to see her, or asking the local police to question her . . . unless, in the meantime, someone decides to talk."

Lapointe went on his way, in the drizzle, with the framed photograph under his arm, while Maigret took a taxi to Boulevard Brune. The apartment house in which the Fabres lived was exactly as he had imagined it: a tall, dull, monotonous building, already shabby-looking, although built only a few years before.

"Dr. Fabre? On the fourth floor, to the right. You'll see a brass plate on his door. If it is Madame Fabre you want, she has just this minute gone out."

She had gone back to her mother's apartment, no doubt, to finish sending out the notices.

He stood motionless in the overly narrow elevator, pressed the bell, and the little maid who came to open the door automatically scanned him right and left, as if she expected to see a child with him.

"Who is it you want?"

"Dr. Fabre."

"These are his office hours."

"Would you be good enough to give him my card. I won't keep him long."

"Come this way, please."

She pushed open the door of the waiting room, filled with half a dozen mothers with children of all ages, and all eyes turned toward him.

He sat down, almost intimidated. There were building blocks on the floor, picture books on a table. One woman was rocking a baby that was becoming almost purple with crying and kept looking at the door to the doctor's office. Maigret knew that they were all wondering:

"Will he be asked to go in ahead of us?"

Because of his presence, nobody talked. The waiting lasted nearly ten minutes, and when the doctor finally opened his office door he turned toward the Superintendent.

He was wearing thick glasses which emphasized the weariness shown in his gaze.

"Come in . . . I'm sorry I can't give you much time. It's not my wife you came to see? She is at her mother's . . ."

"I know."

"Do sit down . . ."

There were baby scales, a glass cupboard full of nickel-plated instruments, a kind of upholstered table covered with a sheet and an oilcloth. Papers were strewn over the desk and books were piled up on the mantelpiece and in a corner right on the floor.

"I'm listening . . ."

"I apologize for disturbing you in the middle of

your appointments, but I didn't know where I could find you alone . . ."

Fabre frowned.

"Why alone?" he asked.

"To tell you the truth, I don't know. I find myself in a most unpleasant situation and it seemed to me you might be able to help me. . . . You go regularly to the home of your in-laws. You therefore know their friends . . ."

"They had very few friends."

"Did you ever meet a man of about forty, dark, and quite good-looking?"

"Who would that be?"

He, too, one would have said was on the defensive.

"I have no idea. I have reason to believe that your father- and mother-in-law both knew a man answering to this general description."

The doctor stared through his glasses at a point in space and Maigret, having given him time to think, finally grew impatient.

"Well?"

As if he was coming out of a trance, Fabre asked:

"What? What do you want to know?"

"Do you know him?"

"I don't know who you are talking about. Almost always when I went to see my parents-in-law it was in the evening, and I used to keep my father-in-law company while the women went to the theater."

"But you know their friends, all the same . . ."

"Some of them . . . Not necessarily all . . ."

"I thought they entertained very little."

"Very little, indeed . . ."

It was exasperating. He looked everywhere but in

the direction of the Superintendent and he seemed to be undergoing a distressing ordeal.

"My wife saw her parents far more often than I did . . . My mother-in-law came here almost every day . . . When I was in my office or at the hospital . . ."

"Did you know that Monsieur Josselin played the horses?"

"No. I thought he hardly ever went out in the afternoon."

"He gambled at the pari-mutuel."

"Oh!"

"His wife, it seems, did not know either. So, he didn't tell her everything . . ."

"Why would he have spoken to *me* about it, when I'm only his son-in-law?"

"Madame Josselin, on her side, hid certain things from her husband."

He did not protest. He seemed to be saying to himself, as one does at the dentist: a few more minutes and it will be over . . .

"One day this week, on Tuesday or Wednesday, she met a man in the afternoon in a brasserie on Boulevard de Montparnasse . . ."

"That's none of my business, is it?"

"Aren't you surprised?"

"I presume she had her reasons for meeting him . . ."

"Monsieur Josselin had met the same man in the morning, in the same brasserie, and seemed to know him well . . . This doesn't mean anything to you?"

The doctor paused before shaking his head wearily.

"Listen carefully, Doctor Fabre. I understand that you may be in a delicate position. Like any man who marries, you are brought into a family you did not previously know and from then on find yourself more or less part of it.

"This family has its little secrets, that's for sure. It is unthinkable that you have not discovered some of them. That was of no significance as long as no crime was committed. But your father-in-law has been murdered and you came quite close to being the suspect."

He said nothing, did not react at all. It was as though they were separated by a glass partition through which their words did not penetrate.

"It is not just a question of a violent crime. A burglar caught in the act of stealing did not kill Monsieur Josselin. It was someone who knew the household as well as you do, its routine, where things were kept. Someone who knew that your wife and her mother were at the theater that night, and that you were probably going to spend the evening with your father-in-law.

"He knew where you live and it was very likely he who telephoned here so that the maid would call you and send you off to Rue Julie . . . Do you agree?"

"It seems plausible . . ."

"You've said yourself that the Josselins rarely entertained and did not have any close friends."

"So I understand."

"Would you be able to swear that you have no idea who that man might be?"

126

The doctor's ears had gone red and he looked more tired than ever.

"Forgive me, Superintendent, but there are children waiting . . ."

"You refuse to talk?"

"If I had some definite information to give you . . ."

"Do you mean that you have some suspicions but not very definite ones?"

"Take it as you please . . . May I remind you that my mother-in-law has just experienced a terrible shock, that she is very emotional even if she does not show her feelings . . ."

Standing up, he went toward the door which opened into the hallway.

"Please don't hold it against me . . ."

He did not hold out his hand but merely said goodby with a nod of the head, and the little maid, who emerged out of the blue, showed the Superintendent out onto the landing.

He was furious, not only with the young pediatrician but with himself, for he felt that he had tackled the problem in the wrong way. Fabre was probably the only member of the family who could have talked, and Maigret had got nothing out of him.

But he had! One thing: Fabre had not even been startled when Maigret had mentioned his mother-in-law meeting with the stranger in the brasserie. It had not surprised him. Moreover, it had not surprised him to learn that Josselin had secretly met the same man in the semi-obscurity of the same brasserie.

He envied Lucas who had already finished with his Polish killer and was doubtless quietly writing up his report.

Maigret kept walking along the sidewalk, on the lookout for taxis which all seemed to be full. The drizzle had turned into a real rain and a glistening jostle of umbrellas could again be seen in the streets.

"If the man met René Josselin and his wife in turn . . ."

He tried to reason it out, but the primary elements were missing. Hadn't the stranger also made contact with the daughter, with Madame Fabre? And why not with Fabre himself?

And why was the whole family protecting him?

"Taxi!"

He finally found an empty one and hurried to get into it.

"Straight ahead . . ."

He still did not know where he was going. His first thought had been to be driven back to the Quai des Orfèvres where he could shut himself up in his office and grumble at his leisure. Hadn't Lapointe, on his part, discovered something new? He felt, without being certain, that the previous concierge no longer lived in Paris, but somewhere in Charente or in central France.

The taxi driver drove slowly, occasionally turning around curiously to look at his passenger.

"What do I do at the traffic light?"

"Turn left . . ."

"As you wish . . ."

And suddenly Maigret leaned forward.

"Drop me off on Rue Dareau."

"Which end of Rue Dareau? It's a long street."

"At the corner of Rue du Saint-Gothard."

"Right . . ."

One by one, Maigret was exhausting all the possibilities. He had to take his notebook out of his pocket to look up Madame Josselin's maiden name: de Lancieux. And he remembered that her father was a retired colonel.

"Excuse me, Madame . . . How long have you been the concierge in this building?"

"Eighteen years, my good man, which doesn't make me any younger."

"You didn't know a retired colonel and his daughter, name de Lancieux, in the neighborhood?"

"Never heard of them . . ."

Two buildings, three buildings. The first concierge, although well on in years, was too young, the second couldn't remember, and the third wasn't more than thirty years old.

"Do you know the number?"

"No. I only know it was near Rue du Saint-Gothard."

"You could ask across the street. The concierge there is at least seventy years old. Speak loudly because she's a little hard of hearing . . ."

He almost shouted. She shook her head.

"No, I don't remember a colonel, but then my memory's not as good as it was. Ever since my husband was run over by a truck I haven't been the same . . ."

He was going to leave, to search elsewhere. She called him back.

"Why don't you ask Mademoiselle Jeanne?"

"Who is she?"

"She's been in this building for at least forty years. She doesn't come down anymore because of her legs. She's on the sixth floor, right at the end of the corridor. The door is never locked. Knock and walk right in. You'll find her in her armchair by the window."

He found her indeed, a small wrinkled old woman but who still had pink cheeks and a childlike smile.

"Lancieux? . . . A colonel? . . . Yes, and how I remember. . . . They lived on the second floor on the left. They had a grouchy maid who lost her temper with all the tradespeople so many times that in the end she had to do her shopping in another neighborhood."

"The colonel had a daughter, didn't he?"

"A young dark-haired girl who wasn't very strong. Her brother wasn't either, poor boy. He was consumptive and had to be sent off to the mountains."

"Are you certain she had a brother?"

"As certain as I see you. And I see you very clearly, despite my age. Don't you want to sit down?"

"You don't know what became of him?"

"Who? The colonel? He put a bullet through his head, and the whole building was upside down because of it. It was the first time such a thing had happened in the neighborhood. He was ill too, it seems he had cancer. But even so I don't approve of him killing himself."

"And his son?"

"What?"

"What became of him?"

"I don't know . . . The last time I saw him was at the funeral."

"Was he younger than his sister?"

"About ten years younger."

"You have never heard anyone mention him?"

"People come and go in a building, you know . . . If I counted the families who have occupied their apartment since then . . . It's the young man you are interested in?"

"He is no longer a young man."

"If he is cured, surely not . . . He is probably married with children of his own . . ."

She added, her eyes sparkling with mischief:

"I have never married and no doubt that's why I shall live to be a hundred . . . You don't believe me? Come back and see me in fifteen years. I promise you I'll still be in this armchair. . . . What do you do for a living?"

Maigret thought it inadvisable to run the risk of giving her a shock by telling her he was from the police, and merely answered, while going for his hat:

"Research . . ."

"In any case it can't be said you don't look far back into the past . . . I bet no one else on the street remembers the de Lancieux now . . . It's something to do with an inheritance, isn't it? Whoever's the heir is lucky you came across me . . . You can tell him. Perhaps he might send me a present . . ."

Half an hour later Maigret was sitting in the office of the coroner, Gossard. He looked relaxed, but rather gloomy. He gave his report in a calm, low voice.

The coroner listened intently, and when Maigret had finished there was quite a long silence during which they could hear the water running along one of the gutters of the Palais de Justice.

131

"What do you plan to do now?"

"Summon them all, this very evening, to the Quai. It will be easier and above all less unpleasant than questioning them at Rue Notre-Dame-des-Champs."

"Do you think they'll talk?"

"One of the three is bound to end up talking . . ."

"Go ahead with your plan."

"Thank you."

"I'd just as soon not be in your shoes. Watch it, though . . . Don't forget that her husband . . ."

"I won't forget, you can be sure of that. That's precisely why I prefer to see them in my office . . ."

One quarter of the Parisians were still on vacation at the beach or in the country. For some the hunting season had started and others were driving along the roads in search of a quiet place to spend the weekend.

Maigret walked slowly along the long, empty corridors and went down to his office.

7

It was five minutes to six. Because it was Saturday most of the offices were empty and there was no activity in the spacious corridor where, right at the end, a solitary man was hanging around outside an office door wondering if he had not been forgotten. The Commissioner of the Police Judiciaire had just left after having come over to shake Maigret's hand.

"Are you going to try this evening?"

"The sooner the better. Tomorrow some of the family may come up from the country; there are probably distant relatives. The funeral is on Monday and I cannot, in all decency, choose that day . . ."

At that point Maigret had already been pacing up and down for an hour in his office, his hands behind his back and smoking pipe after pipe, preparing for what he hoped would be the end of the case. He did not like to call it "setting the scene" but rather "setting the places," as one did in restaurants, and he was always anxious not to forget any details.

At half past five, having given all his instructions, he had gone down to have a beer at the brasserie

Dauphine. It was still raining. It was a dreary day. Actually he drank two glasses of beer one after the other, as though he realized it would be some time before he would have another chance.

When he returned to his office he had only to wait. At last there was a knock at the door and it was Torrence who came in first, looking excited and important, his face flushed as it always was when he was entrusted with a difficult assignment. He carefully pushed the door shut behind him and announced with a look of triumph:

"They are here!"

"In the waiting room?"

"Yes. They are alone. They seemed surprised that you weren't going to see them immediately, especially the mother. I think that annoyed her."

"What happened?"

"When I arrived at the apartment the housekeeper opened the door. I told her who I was and she muttered: 'Again!'

"The door to the living room was shut. I had to wait quite a long time in the hall and I heard some whispering going on but couldn't make out what was being said.

"At last, after a good quarter of an hour, the door opened and I saw a priest being shown to the landing. It was the mother who showed him out.

"She stared at me as though she were trying to recognize me, then asked me to follow her. The daughter was in the living room, and her eyes were red, as if she had just been crying."

"What did she say when she saw the summons?"

"She read it twice. Her hand trembled slightly.

She passed it to her daughter who in turn read it and then looked at her mother as if to say:

" 'I was sure. I warned you . . .'

"All this happened as if in slow motion and I felt uncomfortable.

" 'Do we have to go?'

"I answered yes. The mother persisted:

" 'With you?'

" 'That's to say I have a car down below. But if you would rather take a cab . . .'

"They spoke to each other in almost a whisper, appeared to reach a decision and asked me to wait a few minutes.

"I stayed by myself in the living room for quite a time while they got ready. They called an old woman who was in the dining room and who followed them into a bedroom.

"When they came back they had their hats and coats on and were busy putting on their gloves.

"The housekeeper asked if she should expect them back for dinner. Madame Josselin answered in a strained voice that she did not know . . .

"They got into the back of the car and didn't utter a word the entire trip. I could see the daughter in the rear-view mirror and she seemed to be the more worried of the two. What do I do now?"

"Nothing for the time being. Wait for me in the office."

Next it was Emile's turn, the waiter in the brasserie, who looked much older in a suit and raincoat.

"I'm going to ask you to wait next door."

"It won't take too long, will it, Chief? Saturday evenings are busy and the others will hold it against me if I leave them strapped with all the work . . ."

"Once I call you it will only take a few minutes."

"And I won't need to testify in court? Do you promise?"

"I promise."

An hour earlier Maigret had telephoned Dr. Fabre. The doctor had listened in silence, then said:

"I will do my best to be there at six o'clock. It will depend on my appointments . . ."

He arrived at five past six and must have seen his wife and mother-in-law through the glass walls of the waiting-room as he went by. Maigret had gone to take a look, at a distance, at that room with its green armchairs, where framed photographs of policemen who had died in action decorated three walls.

The electric light in the room was on all day long. The atmosphere was gloomy, depressing. He remembered certain suspects who had been left there for hours, to cool their heels, as if they had been forgotten, in order to break down their resistance.

Madame Josselin sat very straight on a chair, motionless, while her daughter kept getting up and sitting down again.

"Come in, Doctor Fabre . . ."

The doctor, by reason of this summons, was expecting a new development in the case and looked concerned.

"I came as quickly as I could . . ." he said.

He had no hat, no coat or raincoat. He must have left his bag in the car.

"Do sit down . . . I won't keep you long."

Maigret settled down at his desk opposite him, took time to light his pipe which he had just filled and said in a soft voice, with a note of reproach:

"Why did you not tell me that your wife has an uncle?"

Fabre must have been expecting it, but all the same his ears turned scarlet, as they always did at the least excitement.

"You didn't ask me . . ." he replied, trying to withstand the gaze of the Superintendent.

"I asked you to tell me who used to come to your in-laws' apartment . . ."

"He did not visit."

"Does that mean you have never seen him?"

"Yes."

"He wasn't at your wedding?"

"No. I know of his existence because my wife has spoken to me about him, but there was never any question of his being at Rue Notre-Dame-des-Champs, in any case not when I was there."

"Be frank, Doctor Fabre . . . When you learned that your father-in-law was dead, that he had been murdered, when you knew that his own gun had been used and that consequently someone who was familiar with the apartment was involved, did you immediately think of him?"

"Not immediately."

"What made you think of him?"

"The attitude of my mother-in-law and my wife . . ."

"Did your wife talk to you about it afterward, when you were by yourselves?"

He took time to think.

"We have been alone very little since this happened."

"She did not tell you anything?"

"She told me that she was frightened . . ."

"Of what?"

"She did not say exactly. She was thinking particularly of her mother . . . I am only a son-in-law. They certainly wanted to accept me into the family but I am not completely part of it. My father-in-law was very generous with me. Madame Josselin adores my children. All the same, there are certain things which do not concern me . . ."

"Do you think that your wife's uncle has not set foot in the apartment since your marriage?"

"All I know is that there was a quarrel, that they felt sorry for him but could no longer have him in their house, for reasons which I did not attempt to go into . . . My wife spoke of him as a wreck, more to be pitied than blamed, a sort of semi-lunatic . . ."

"Is that all you know?"

"That's all. Are you going to question Madame Josselin?"

"It's my duty."

"Please do not be too harsh with her. She appears self-controlled. Some people are deceived and take her for rather a hard woman. I know, however, that she is extremely sensitive but unable to show her emotions. Since the death of her husband, I have been expecting her nerves to give way at any moment . . ."

"I will treat her with all possible consideration."

"Thank you . . . Is that all?"

"I give you back to your patients . . ."

"May I have a word with my wife as I go out?"

"I would rather you did not speak to her and especially not to your mother-in-law."

"In that case, tell her that if I am not at home when she gets back, I'll be at the hospital . . . I got a call just as I was leaving and I will probably have to operate."

Just as he was about to reach the door he changed his mind and came back.

"I apologize for having been so reticent . . . Think of my position. I have been generously welcomed into a family which is not my own. This family, like others, has its misfortunes. I did not think it was for me to . . ."

"I understand, Doctor Fabre . . ."

A good man, too, of course! More than just a good man, probably, according to those who knew him, and this time the two men shook hands.

Maigret went over and opened the door of the Inspectors' Room and brought Emile into his office.

"What do I have to do?"

"Nothing. Stay there, by the window. I'll probably ask you a question and you will answer me . . ."

"Even if it's not the answer you are expecting?"

"You will tell the truth . . ."

Maigret went to get Madame Josselin, who stood up at the same time as her daughter.

"If you will follow me . . . Just you . . . I will see Madame Fabre presently . . ."

She was wearing a black dress lightly flecked with gray, a black hat trimmed with a few small white feathers, and a light camel's-hair coat.

Maigret had her walk ahead of him and she saw at once the man standing by the window, awkwardly twisting his hat in his hands. She looked surprised, turned toward the Superintendent and, as no one spoke, finally asked:

"Who is this?"

"Don't you recognize him?"

She looked at him more closely and shook her head.

"No . . ."

"And what about you, Emile, do you recognize this lady?"

In a voice hoarse with emotion, the waiter answered:

"Yes, Superintendent. It is definitely her."

"Is she the person who came into the brasserie Franco-Italienne at the beginning of the week, during the afternoon, and joined a man of about forty? Are you certain?"

"She was wearing the same dress and the same hat . . . I mentioned them to you this morning . . ."

"Thank you. You can go."

Emile looked at Madame Josselin as though he wished to apologize for what he had done.

"You won't need me any more?"

"I don't think so."

They remained alone, to talk in private. Maigret pointed to an armchair opposite his desk and walked behind the desk but did not sit down.

"Do you know where your brother is?" he asked in a quiet voice.

She looked straight at him with her dark, bright eyes, as she had done at Rue Notre-Dame-des-Champs, but she was not so tense and one even

140

sensed a certain relief within her. This was even more noticeable when she decided to sit down. It was rather as if she finally agreed to abandon a certain attitude which she had struggled reluctantly to maintain.

"What did my son-in-law tell you?" she asked, replying to one question with another.

"Very little. . . . He only confirmed that you have a brother, which I already knew . . ."

"Who told you?"

"A very old lady nearly ninety who still lives in the building on Rue Dareau where you used to live with your father and brother . . ."

"It was bound to happen . . ." she forced out.

He came back to the point.

"Do you know where he is?"

She shook her head.

"No. And I swear I am telling you the truth. Up until last Wednesday I was even convinced he was miles from Paris . . ."

"He never wrote to you?"

"Not since he no longer came to our house . . ."

"Did you realize at once that it was he who had killed your husband?"

"I am still not sure . . . I refuse to believe it . . . I know that everything is against him . . ."

"Why, by your own silence and by forcing your daughter to be silent, did you try to save him come what may?"

"At first, because he is my brother and because he is unhappy. Then, because to some extent I feel somewhat responsible myself . . ."

She took a handkerchief out of her handbag but

did not use it to wipe her eyes which remained dry and still shining with an inner intensity. Mechanically, she rolled it into a ball with her thin fingers while she was talking or awaiting the Superintendent's questions.

"Now I am ready to tell you everything."

"What is your brother's name?"

"Philippe . . . Philippe de Lancieux. He is eight years younger than I."

"Unless I am mistaken, he spent part of his adolescence in a mountain sanatorium?"

"Not his adolescence . . . he was only five when it was discovered that he had contracted tuberculosis. The doctors sent him to the Haute-Savoie where he stayed until he was twelve."

"Your mother had already died?"

"She died a few days after he was born. And that explains a great deal . . . I suppose everything I am about to tell you will be all over the newspapers tomorrow . . ."

"I promise you nothing will be in the papers. What does your mother's death explain?"

"The attitude of my father toward Philippe and plainly his behavior during the second part of his life. From the day my mother died he was a changed man, and I am sure he always held it against Philippe, in spite of himself; he thought him responsible for the death of his wife . . .

"On top of this, he began to drink. . . . It was about this time that he resigned from the army, although he had virtually no income, and so we lived very poorly . . ."

"While your brother was in the mountains, were you alone with your father on Rue Dareau?"

"We had an elderly maid staying with us—she's dead now."

"And when Philippe returned?"

"My father sent him to a Catholic school in Montmorency and we hardly saw him except on vacations. He ran away when he was fourteen and was found two days later at Le Havre. He had got there by hitch-hiking.

"He told people that he had to reach Le Havre in a hurry because his mother was dying. Already then he was making up stories . . . he would invent some tale or other and people would believe him because he ended up believing it himself . . .

"Since the school at Montmorency did not want him back my father placed him in another institution, near Versailles.

"He was still there when I met René Josselin . . . I was twenty-two . . ."

The handkerchief was now twisted into a cord that she pulled through her clenched hands; Maigret, without realizing it, had let his pipe go out.

"Then I made a mistake and I have always reproached myself for it . . . I thought only of myself . . ."

"Did you hesitate to marry?"

She stared at him, at a loss for the right words.

"This is the first time I have had to speak of these things, which I have always kept to myself. Life with my father had become even more difficult; though I didn't know it, he was already ill. I realized, however, that he was not going to live for many more years, that sooner or later Philippe would need me. You see, I never should have married . . . I said so to René . . ."

"Did you have a job?"

"My father would not allow it. He thought that an office was not the right place for a young girl. But I considered taking a job, and living later with my brother. René was insistent . . . He was thirty-five, he was in his prime, and I trusted him completely.

"He told me that whatever happened he would look after Philippe, that he would consider him as his own son, and at last I gave in . . .

"I shouldn't have . . . It was the easy way out . . . Overnight, I escaped from the oppressive atmosphere of the house and got rid of my responsibilities . . .

"I had a feeling . . ."

"Did you love your husband?"

She looked him straight in the eye and said with a kind of defiance in her voice:

"Yes, Chief Superintendent . . . And I loved him until the end . . . He was the man . . ."

For the first time her voice broke a little and she turned her head away for a moment.

"Nonetheless, I have thought all my life that I should have made a sacrifice . . . Two months after we were married when the doctor told me my father had incurable cancer, I looked on it as a punishment . . ."

"Did you tell your husband this?"

"No. Everything I am telling you today I am saying for the first time, because it is the only way, if

144

my brother has really done what you believe, of pleading his cause . . . If necessary I will repeat it all in court . . . Contrary to what you may think, I do not care about people's opinions . . ."

She had become agitated and fidgeted more and more with her hands. She opened her handbag again and took out a small metal box.

"Would you by any chance have a glass of water? . . . I better take some medicine which Dr. Larue prescribed for me . . ."

Maigret went over to open the cupboard in which there was a faucet, a glass, and even a bottle of cognac which sometimes came in handy.

"Thank you . . . I am trying to keep calm. Everyone has always thought of me as being very self-controlled, without having any idea of what an effort it is to give this impression . . . What was I saying?"

"You were talking about your marriage. Your brother was then at Versailles . . . Your father . . ."

"Yes . . . My brother only stayed one year at Versailles. He was expelled."

"Had he tried to run away again?"

"No, but he was unruly and his teachers couldn't do anything with him. You see, I have never lived long enough with him to really know him . . . I am sure he is not bad at heart. It's his imagination which plays nasty tricks on him.

"Perhaps it all started in his childhood in the sanatorium, where he was in bed most of the time, isolated from the world, as it were.

"I remember something he said to me one day when I found him lying on the floor in the attic,

145

while we had been looking everywhere for him.

" 'What are you doing here, Philippe?'

" 'I'm telling myself stories . . .'

"Unfortunately he told them to other people too. I suggested to my father that he come to live with us. René was willing. It was even he who suggested it first. My father did not want us to have him and stuck him in another school, in Paris this time.

"Philippe came to see us every week on Rue Notre-Dame-des-Champs, where we were already living. My husband really looked upon him as his son. However, Véronique was born . . ."

A calm, peaceful street, a cozy apartment surrounded by convents, a stone's throw from the shade of the Luxembourg Gardens. Good people. A prosperous business. A happy family . . .

"My father shot himself, as you know . . ."

"Where did this happen?"

"On Rue Dareau. In his armchair. He had put on his uniform and placed a portrait of my mother and of me in front of him. Not one of Philippe . . ."

"What became of Philippe?"

"He continued his studies as best he could. We kept him for two years at home. It was obvious he would never pass his final exams and René intended to take him into his business."

"How did your husband and brother get on?"

"René had endless patience. He kept Philippe's escapades from me as much as possible and Philippe took advantage of this. He could not bear any kind of restriction, any discipline. Often we would not see him at meals and he would come home at all hours, always with some fine story to tell us . . .

"War broke out. Philippe was expelled from one last school, and my husband and I, without admitting it to each other, were both increasingly worried about him.

"I think René also felt a kind of remorse. . . . Perhaps if I had stayed on Rue Dareau . . ."

"I don't think so," said Maigret gravely. "You must tell yourself that your marriage did not have any influence on the way things developed."

"Do you think so?"

"In my work I have met dozens of people in the same state as your brother, who did not have his excuses for their conduct."

She wanted to believe him but still could not quite bring herself to it.

"What happened during the war?"

"Philippe was bent on enlisting. He was just eighteen and he was so persistent that we finally gave in.

"In May 1940 he was taken prisoner in the Ardennes and for a long time we were without any news from him.

"He spent the whole war in Germany, first in a camp and then on a farm near Munich . . .

"We hoped he would be a different man when he returned."

"He remained the same?"

"Physically, he was indeed a man, and I hardly recognized him. The outdoor life had done him good and he had become robust, sturdy. But as soon as he began describing his experiences we realized that at heart he was still the boy who ran away and made up stories . . .

"To hear him talking, he had been through the

most extraordinary adventures. He had escaped three or four times, in fantastic circumstances . . .

"He had lived, which is possible, as husband with the woman on whose farm he was working and he claimed he had two children by her. She had another by her husband . . .

"The husband, according to Philippe, had been killed at the Russian front. My brother spoke of returning, of marrying the farmer's wife and staying in Germany for good . . .

"Then, a month later, he had other plans. America tempted him and he claimed he had got to know secret service agents who would welcome him with open arms."

"He wasn't working?"

"My husband had given him a job at Rue du Saint-Gothard, as he had promised . . ."

"Did he live with you?"

"He stayed with us only three weeks before moving into a place near Saint-Germain-des-Pres where he lived with a waitress. He again talked of marrying. Each time he had a new love-affair he made plans to marry . . .

" 'She's expecting a baby, you see, and I'd be a swine if I didn't marry her.'

"I've lost count of the children he claims to have had here, there, and everywhere . . ."

"It wasn't true?"

"My husband tried to find out. He never obtained convincing proof. Each time it was a way of extracting money from him.

"And I soon discovered he was playing the same game with us both. He came to me with his secrets, begged me to help him. Each time, he needed a certain sum of money to get him out of trouble, after which all would be well."

"Did you give him what he wanted?"

"I nearly always gave in. He knew I didn't have much money at my disposal. My husband never refused me anything. He gave me what I needed for the house and did not ask for accounts. All the same, I would not have been able to give away large amounts without speaking to him about it . . .

"So, cunningly, Philippe would approach René in secret. . . . He would tell him the same story, or another one, begging him not to tell me about it."

"How did your brother come to leave Rue du Saint-Gothard?"

"We discovered irregularities. It was all the more serious as he used to approach important clients and ask them for payments in my husband's name."

"And your husband finally lost his temper?"

"He had a long talk with him. Instead of giving him a fixed sum to get rid of him, he arranged with his bank to pay Philippe a monthly allowance, enough for him to live on . . . I suppose you can guess what happened next?"

"He started in again . . ."

"And each time we forgave him. Each time he really gave us the impression that he was going to make a fresh start. . . . We welcomed him back. . . . Then he disappeared, after having done something unscrupulous again. . . .

"For a while he lived in Bordeaux. He swears he married there, that there is a child, a daughter, but if this is true—and we never had any proof apart from a

photograph of a woman who might have been anybody—if this is true, as I said, he soon left his wife
and daughter and went off to settle in Brussels . . .

"There, still according to him, he would have
been thrown into prison if my husband didn't send
him some money. . . . He did.

"I don't know if you understand. . . . It's difficult
without knowing him. . . . He always seemed sincere and I wonder if he wasn't. . . . He is not really
bad. . . ."

"He did kill your husband, you know."

"As long as there is no proof and as long as he does
not confess to it, I shall refuse to believe it. And I
shall always have doubts . . . I shall always wonder
whether it wasn't my fault. . . ."

"How long ago did he stop coming to Rue Notre-
Dame-des-Champs?"

"You mean to the apartment?"

"I don't understand the distinction."

"Because he hasn't actually set foot in the house
for at least seven years. That was after Brussels, before Marseilles, when Véronique was still single. Up
until then he had always looked handsome, for he
was very elegant and careful of his appearance. We
saw him come back looking almost like a tramp and
it was obvious that he had not had enough to
eat . . .

"Never had he appeared so humble, so repentant.
We kept him at home for a few days and, as he
claimed he had a job waiting for him in Gabon, my
husband again gave him a helping hand . . .

"We heard nothing more from him for nearly two
years. Then, one morning when I went out shopping,

150

I found him waiting for me on the sidewalk at the corner of the street . . .

"I won't go into his new stories . . . I gave him some money . . .

"This happened several times in the course of the last few years. He swore to me that he had not approached René, that he would never ask him for anything again . . ."

"And, the very same day, he arranged to see him?"

"Yes. As I said, he continued to play both games. I've had proof of this since yesterday."

"How?"

"I had a feeling . . . I suspected that one day you would discover the existence of Philippe and would ask me explicit questions . . ."

"You were hoping that would be as late as possible so that he would have time to get out of the country?"

"Wouldn't you have done the same? Do you think your wife, for example, would not have done the same thing?"

"He killed your husband."

"Even if we assume that this is proven, he is still my brother, and putting him in prison for the rest of his life won't bring René back. *I* know Philippé. . . . But if, one day, I have to tell a jury what I have just told you, they will not believe me. . . . He is a wretched soul rather than a criminal."

What was the use of discussing it with her? And it was true, to a certain extent, that Philippe de Lancieux was marked by fate.

"I was saying that I went through my husband's papers, in particular his old checkbooks. There were

151

two drawers full, carefully arranged, as he was meticulous . . .

"This was how I discovered that, each time Philippe had come to see me, he had also gone to see my husband, first at Rue du Saint-Gothard and later somewhere else. He probably waited in the street for him, as he waited for me."

"Your husband never spoke to you about it?"

"He was afraid of upsetting me. And I him. If we had been more open with each other perhaps nothing would have happened . . . I've thought a great deal about it. . . . On Wednesday, shortly before noon, while René was still out, the telephone rang and I immediately recognized Philippe's voice."

Wasn't he telephoning from the brasserie Franco-Italienne, where Josselin had only just left him? Probably. It could be verified. Perhaps the cashier would remember having given him a token.

"He told me he absolutely had to see me, that it was a matter of life or death, and that afterwards we would never hear of him again. . . . As you know, he arranged to meet me in that brasserie. I met him there on my way to the hairdresser."

"Just a minute. Did you tell your brother you were going to the hairdresser?"

"Yes . . . I wanted to explain to him why I was in such a hurry."

"And you spoke of going to the theater?"

"Wait . . . I am almost sure . . . I must have said to him:

" 'I must go to the hairdresser because I'm going to the theater with Véronique tonight.'

"He seemed even more anxious than on the previous occasions. . . . He admitted that he had done something very foolish, he didn't say what, but gave me to understand that he might be arrested by the police. He needed a large sum of money in order to board a ship for South America. I had put all the money available to me in my handbag and I gave it to him . . .

"I don't understand why, in the evening, he would have come to our home to kill my husband . . ."

"Did he know that the gun was in the drawer?"

"It has been kept there for at least fifteen years, probably longer, and at that time Philippe sometimes lived with us, as I told you."

"Naturally he also knew where the key was kept in the kitchen."

"He didn't take any money. For there was some money in my husband's wallet and it wasn't touched. There was also some money in the desk and jewelry in my bedroom."

"Did your husband make out a check to Philippe on the day he died?"

"No."

There was a hush while they looked at each other.

"I think," sighed Maigret, "that this is the explanation."

"My husband would have refused?"

"It's likely . . ."

Or had he perhaps merely given his brother-in-law some cash he had in his pocket?

"Did your husband always carry his checkbook?"

If he didn't, he might have arranged to meet Philippe in the evening.

"He always had it in his pocket."

In that case, it was Lancieux who, having failed in the morning, had started up again. Had he already decided to kill? Was he hoping, with his sister being in charge of the money in the future, that he would manage to get more out of her?

Maigret did not attempt to pursue his guesswork further. He had found out all he could about the characters, and the rest would one day be up to the judges.

"You don't know if he had been in Paris a long time?"

"I swear to you that I haven't the slightest idea. Admittedly, all I hope for is that he has had time to leave the country and that we won't hear of him again."

"And if, one day, he again begged you for some money? If you received a telegram, from Brussels for instance, from Switzerland or elsewhere, asking you to send him a money order?"

"I don't think . . ."

She did not finish her sentence. For the first time she looked down to avoid Maigret's eyes and stammered:

"You don't believe me either."

This time there was a long silence and the Superintendent fiddled with one of his pipes, decided to fill and light it, as he had not dared to do so during the conversation.

They had nothing more to say to each other, that was evident. Madame Josselin opened her handbag once more to put back her handkerchief, and the clasp snapped shut with a sharp click. It was like a signal. After one last moment of hesitation she stood up, not as stiff as when she had come in.

"You do not require me further?"

"Not for the time being."

"I suppose you will get the police to search for him?"

He merely looked down. Then, walking toward the door, he remarked:

"I don't even have a photograph of him."

"I know you won't believe me, but I haven't got one either, apart from photos which date from before the war, when he was a boy."

Standing in front of the door which Maigret half opened, they were both rather embarrassed, as if they did not know how to say good-by.

"Are you going to question my daughter?"

"It's no longer necessary . . ."

"I think perhaps she has suffered the most these last few days . . . My son-in-law too, I suppose. They didn't have the same reasons for keeping silent . . . they did it for me."

"I don't hold it against them . . ."

He held out his hand hesitantly and she placed her hand in his, having just put her gloves back on.

"I will not say good luck . . ." she muttered.

And without turning around again she walked toward the glass-enclosed waiting-room, where an anxious Véronique jumped to her feet.

8

Winter had come and gone. Ten, twenty times, the lights had stayed on, late in the evening and even far into the night. Each time this meant that a man or a woman was sitting in the armchair which Madame Josselin had occupied, opposite Maigret's desk.

The description of Philippe de Lancieux had been sent to all branches of the police and searches were carried out at railway stations, as well as at border-crossings and in the airports. Interpol had produced a poster which was given to the police in other countries.

It was not until the end of March, however, when the tops of the chimneys looked pink against the pale blue sky and buds were beginning to burst forth, that Maigret, arriving at his office one morning, without an overcoat for the first time that year, again heard news of Madame Josselin's brother.

Madame Josselin was still living in the apartment on Rue Notre-Dame-des-Champs, with a kind of companion; she still went every afternoon to see her grandchildren on Boulevard Brune and to take them for walks in Montsouris Park.

Philippe de Lancieux had just been found dead, stabbed several times with a knife, at about three o'clock in the morning, near a bar on Avenue des Ternes.

The newspapers wrote: *Crime in the Underworld.*

This was, as always, more or less the case. Though Lancieux had never belonged to the underworld, he had nonetheless been living for some months with a prostitute named Angèle.

He was still inventing stories and Angèle was convinced that if he was hiding in her room and only going out at night, it was because he had escaped from Fontevrault where he was serving a twenty-year sentence.

Had others realized that he was mentally defective? Had he been punished for having taken the young woman away from her rightful protector?

An inquiry was opened, rather half-heartedly, as was usually the case in circumstances like this. Maigret had to go once more to Rue Notre-Dame-des-Champs; he again saw the concierge whose baby was sitting in a high chair and babbling away, went up to the third floor and pressed the bell.

Madame Manu was still working a few hours each day in the apartment and it was she who opened the door, this time sliding back the chain.

"It's you!" she said, frowning, as if he could only be the bearer of bad news.

But was the news so bad?

Nothing had altered in the living room, except for

a blue scarf which was draped over René Josselin's armchair.

"I'll go and tell Madame . . ."

"Thank you."

But he still felt the need to mop his brow as he glanced at himself in the mirror.